THE GUNSMITH

286

THE GHOST OF GOLIAD

J. R. ROBERTS

JOVE BOOKS, NEW YORK

THE BERKLEY PUBLISHING GROUP
Published by the Penguin Group
Penguin Group (USA) Inc.
375 Hudson Street, New York, New York 10014, USA
Penguin Group (Canada), 90 Eglinton Avenue East, Suite 700, Toronto, Ontario M4P 2Y3, Canada
(a division of Pearson Penguin Canada Inc.)
Penguin Books Ltd., 80 Strand, London WC2R 0RL, England
Penguin Group Ireland, 25 St. Stephen's Green, Dublin 2, Ireland (a division of Penguin Books Ltd.)
Penguin Group (Australia), 250 Camberwell Road, Camberwell, Victoria 3124, Australia
(a division of Pearson Australia Group Pty. Ltd.)
Penguin Books India Pvt. Ltd., 11 Community Centre, Panchsheel Park, New Delhi—110 017, India
Penguin Group (NZ), Cnr. Airborne and Rosedale Roads, Albany, Auckland 1310, New Zealand
(a division of Pearson New Zealand Ltd.)
Penguin Books (South Africa) (Pty.) Ltd., 24 Sturdee Avenue, Rosebank, Johannesburg 2196,
South Africa

Penguin Books Ltd., Registered Offices: 80 Strand, London WC2R 0RL, England

THE GHOST OF GOLIAD

A Jove Book / published by arrangement with the author

PRINTING HISTORY
Jove edition / October 2005

ISBN: 0-515-14020-1

JOVE®
Jove Books are published by The Berkley Publishing Group,
a division of Penguin Group (USA) Inc.,
375 Hudson Street, New York, New York 10014.
JOVE is a registered trademark of Penguin Group (USA) Inc.
The "J" design is a trademark belonging to Penguin Group (USA) Inc.

PRINTED IN THE UNITED STATES OF AMERICA

10 9 8 7 6 5 4 3 2 1

CIVIC PRIDE

"Look," Clint said harshly, "I don't want one of your whores. Is that clear enough?"

The big man took a step back, as if Clint had struck him across the face.

"What, our whores ain't good enough for you?"

"Jesus . . . " Clint said, at a loss as to what to say next to get the man to leave him alone.

"Hey, boys," the man shouted, "this feller says that Gonzales whores ain't good enough for him."

"I didn't say that—"

Clint was interrupted by the sound of chairs sliding across the floor as the other men in the place stood up. He looked around and found a dozen men scowling at him the way the bartender had been, and these men were armed.

Apparently, the men of Gonzales, Texas, took great pride in their whores.

ONE

In all the years he'd spent in Texas, Clint Adams had never once been to the site of the Alamo.

It had been more than fifty years since two hundred brave men had died, holding off Santa Anna's force of over thirteen hundred men as long as they could before they succumbed to the superior numbers. The names of the men who had died there were legend—Travis, Bowie, Crockett—but Clint knew firsthand how legends grew out of proportion to the attributes of the real man.

As he rode into the town of Gonzales, Texas, this was the closest he had ever come to the Alamo. The two towns the mission had drawn volunteers from had been Gonzales and Goliad, which had been roughly equidistant from there.

Gonzales had fallen on hard times, he noticed, unless this was what the town had looked like all those years ago. Many of the buildings had started out as abode structures, but the walls had started crumbling years ago, to be replaced with wood. Now they resembled odd hybrids of what they had once been and what they now were.

1

The good thing about a town this size, it was easy to find the hotel and livery. There was only one of each. Attached to the hotel was a cantina, so after Clint boarded his horse and checked into his room, he went into the cantina for a drink and some food. There were a few men in the place, and they were all Mexican. In fact, the food the place offered was all Mexican, as well.

"Tortillas," the bartender said, "enchiladas, beans. That's all we got."

"Well then, that's what I'll have," Clint said, "and a beer."

"Comin' up."

The bartender—who was Anglo, not Mexican—brought him the beer and said, "Have a seat. I'll have the girl bring it out to you."

"Thanks."

Clint took a table against the wall and sipped his beer. This was the day he was supposed to meet Elizabeth Vargas and her father, but apparently they hadn't arrived yet. All he had to do, though, was sit and wait. The proposition Elizabeth had made to him in Labyrinth was too interesting to pass up . . . in more ways than one . . .

She had appeared in Labyrinth one day, asking about him at Rick's Saloon. His friend Rick Hartman had sent word to the hotel that someone was looking for him, but it wasn't until he arrived that he found out who it was.

"Right there," Rick said, with a jerk of his chin.

Elizabeth Vargas made Clint's breath catch in his throat. She had a mane of curly black hair that made her alabaster skin seem even paler. She was seated, but he could see from her long legs that she was tall. She was wearing a blood-red shirt that made her full, round breasts seem even larger. All in all she was a larger-than-life woman, the kind who attracted attention from men and women alike. It was also of great interest to him that she was wearing a gun.

It was early, and there were only a few men in the saloon, but they were all staring longingly at the woman.

"And she asked for me?"

"Believe me," Rick said, "I wouldn't have sent for you if she hadn't. I'd be over there, myself."

Clint noticed she had an almost empty mug of beer in front of her. Another point in her favor.

"Give me two fresh beers, Rick."

"Comin' up."

Clint carried the two mugs with him to the woman's table and set them down.

"Clint Adams?" she asked, her black eyes widening as she looked up at him.

"That's right," he said. He sat across from her. "I brought you a fresh beer."

"*Gracias.*"

She pushed away the remnants of the old one and pulled the new one to her. Her voice was low and throaty, with just the faintest hint of Mexican accent.

"You speak English very well."

"My mother was American," she said. "My father is Mexican."

"She's dead?"

"Yes."

"But he still lives."

"He is very old."

"Where is he?"

"Right now he is in Mexico, but soon he will be in Gonzales. We are supposed to meet him there."

"We are?" he asked. "How is it I don't know anything about this meeting?"

"I have come here to arrange it, Señor Adams." She leaned forward, placing her elbows on the table.

"Is that a fact?"

"I have come to ask you for your help," she said.

"For you?"

"For me," she said, "for my father . . . and for my family."

TWO

Clint had nothing better to do that day than sit in a saloon and have a beer with a beautiful woman, so he sat back and said, "Why don't you tell me what it is you think I can do to help your family, Elizabeth?"

"My father," Elizabeth said, "he was at the Alamo."

Now Clint sat forward, interested. "That was a long time ago."

"Yes," she said. "He is . . . seventy-eight years old."

"Does this have something to do with the Alamo?" Clint asked.

"Yes."

"Does he know what happened there?"

"He knows everything," she said, with a shrug. "He was there."

An opportunity to talk with someone who was at the Alamo. Clint didn't know if he could pass that up. He took a drink from his beer mug, taking a moment to think. Before he could ask another question, though, Elizabeth continued.

"My father needs help," she said. "He asked me to come and talk to you."

5

"Why me?"

"He knows your reputation," she said, "and he knew that you would be here."

"Here? In Texas? Or in Labyrinth?"

"Both."

"And how did he know that?"

"My father knows many things," she said. "In Mexico he is a wealthy man. He has many eyes and ears."

"Including yours."

"Yes," she said, with a nod, "including mine."

Clint put his beer down. "Where is your father now?"

"In Mexico."

"And does he want me to go there and talk to him?"

"No," she said. "He said to tell you he will meet with you in Gonzales."

"Gonzales? Is that in Texas?"

"Yes. It was the town nearest to the Alamo. That and Goliad are where your Colonel Bowie collected his volunteers."

"When are we to meet?"

"In one week."

"Will you be there?"

"I will be with my father, yes."

"Why so long from now?"

"I need time to return to Mexico and give my father your answer, then make arrangements to take my father to Gonzales."

"Take him?"

"He cannot ride anymore."

"I see."

"Of course," she said, "that will be only if you agree to meet with him."

"Well," Clint said, "I'll have to give it some thought."

She looked disappointed.

"How long?" she asked. "I must return home with your answer as soon as—"

"Give me until the end of today," he said. "I'll make up my mind by then. Where are you staying?"

"The hotel down the street."

"The Labyrinth House?"

"Yes, that is the one."

"I'll come and talk to you there."

She looked uncertain about what to do next, then said, "Very well," and stood up. "Tonight, at my hotel."

"Tonight," he said.

She nodded and left the saloon, all male eyes following her to the door. Once she was gone, Rick Hartman came out from behind the bar and joined Clint at the table.

"What did she want?" he asked.

Clint told him.

"That's all?" Rick asked. "She just wants you to go to Gonzales and talk to her father?"

"That's it, so far."

"She didn't tell you what it's about?"

"No."

"How about money?"

"What?"

"Did she offer you any money?"

Clint frowned. "Come to think of it, she didn't."

"And you didn't ask?"

"She did say her father is very wealthy," Clint said, "but, Rick, you saw her."

"Yes, I saw her," Rick said, shaking his head. "I guess I don't blame you for not thinkin' to ask about money. Are you gonna go?"

"I don't know," Clint said. "It's tempting, you know? To talk to someone who was actually at the Alamo?"

"Maybe," Rick said.

"Maybe?"

"Well, think about it," he said. "He's only gonna tell you the Mexican side of the story, isn't he?"

"Like you said," Clint replied. "Maybe."

THREE

Clint had gone directly from Rick's Saloon to the hotel where Elizabeth was staying. She was surprised when she opened the door and saw him standing there.

"You have come so soon? It has only been an hour."

"We need to talk about this some more," Clint said.

"You are interested?"

"I'm interested, but I have more questions. Will you come downstairs to the hotel dining room with me?"

"I suppose I am hungry," she said. "Very well. We will eat and talk more. Perhaps that will help you make up your mind."

"Perhaps," he agreed.

When they were seated in the dining room and had given the waiter their order, Clint said, "You said something about your father being wealthy?"

"Yes."

"Does that mean that he's willing to pay me for what he wants me to do?"

"Pay you?" She frowned.

9

"Didn't he say anything about paying me?"

"The stories we heard of The Gunsmith," she said, "did not say anything about paying you."

It was true Clint had money in a number of banks from businesses and mines he had a percentage of in different parts of the country, but that didn't mean that he enjoyed working for free. He liked to be paid when he could.

"Okay," he said, "never mind that for now. Why don't you tell me exactly what your father wants me to do?"

"He told me that he wanted to be the one to tell you," she said. "I was simply to ask you to come to Gonzales to speak with him."

"Do you even know what he wants to talk to me about?" Clint asked. "Has he confided in you?"

She looked startled.

"Of course he confides in me," she said. "He loves me, and I him."

"Elizabeth . . . do you have any siblings?"

"Siblings?"

"Brothers or sisters?"

"No," she said. "I was my parents' only child."

"You carry a gun," he said, "and dress like a man, but you are very much a woman—a beautiful woman."

"Thank you," she said. "My father wanted a son very badly. I am afraid I have spent years trying to be like a son to him."

The waiter came with their food at that point and they fell silent, sat back and allowed him to serve it. When the smell of the steaks hit them, they both realized how hungry they were, and bent to the task of eating . . .

Clint's thoughts were brought back to the present in Gonzales when a Mexican girl appeared with his food. She appeared to be about sixteen, a lovely little thing with very black hair and budding breasts. She reminded him of Elizabeth Vargas, only ten years younger.

"Thank you."

"Con mucho gusto, señor," the girl said, with a slight curtsy. "Do you wish me to come to your room tonight? Only one dollar."

"To my room—no," he said, "that won't be necessary."

She pouted. "You do not like me? You do not think I am pretty, or desirable?"

"You are both pretty and desirable," he assured her.

"Then I will come to you tonight," she said, happily. "Only one dollar."

"What's your name?" he asked.

"Raquel."

"Raquel, I would like to eat my food now, and I do not want you to come to my room tonight, but thank you."

She pouted again, and walked sadly away.

Clint picked up his fork and cut into his enchiladas, letting his mind float back to the steaks he'd shared with Elizabeth, and the startling fact she finally revealed to him . . .

They spoke very little as they ate, but once the steaks were polished off and they had coffee and pie in front of them, Clint tried to pick the conversation up from where they had left off.

"Elizabeth," he said, "I think before I can agree to ride to Gonzales, without even knowing if I'm going to be paid anything or not, I need to know exactly what the job is."

"My father did not describe it as a job," she said. "He called it a . . . a task."

"Very well," he said. "What is the task?"

"He will be angry if I tell you."

"Not if by telling me you convince me to go to Gonzales," he reasoned.

She thought a moment, the nodded and said, "*Bien,* that is good logic."

"Thank you."

"There is a man in Goliad my father wishes you to visit, to find out if he is who he says he is."

"And who does this man say he is?"

"He is very old, my father's age," she said, "and he claims to be Captain William Travis, of the Alamo."

"But . . . Travis died at the Alamo, along with Bowie and Crockett and all the others, more than fifty years ago."

"Indeed," she said, "and my father watched him die . . . or so he thinks. He now needs you to confirm this for him."

"Why doesn't your father go to Goliad and confirm it himself?" Clint asked, still reeling from the news.

"Because this man Travis controls Goliad," she said. "There he is known as the Ghost of Goliad, and everyone lives in fear of him and his men. If my father shows his face there, this Travis—or whoever he is—will have him killed."

Clint sat back in his chair and digested this information. A man claiming to be Travis of the Alamo . . . or his ghost . . . this was certainly something that was hard to pass up.

"Señor Adams—"

"Clint," he said, interrupting her, "just call me Clint."

"Clint . . . will you agree to meet with my father in Gonzales one week from today?"

"All right, Elizabeth," he said, picking up his coffee cup and raising it to her, "I will meet with him."

FOUR

And so here he sat, in the cantina in Gonzales, consuming what turned out to be very good Mexican food, waiting to meet with a man known as Don Carlos Miguel Santa Ynez Vargas and his beautiful daughter, Elizabeth.

When Clint walked Elizabeth back to her hotel room that last night she was in Labyrinth, he had been tempted to try to stay with her, but in the end he played the perfect gentleman and stopped at her door. He could not tell whether this had disappointed her or pleased her as she bade him good night, but he had regretted it later and now hoped to correct that error as soon as possible.

While he was finishing his food, the bartender came over to him and stood before his table, arms folded. He was a big man, with thick, sturdy legs and muscular arms, and he was scowling. Clint hated when men this man's size scowled. It was always a bad sign. The only good sign was that the man was not armed.

"You insulted my girl," the man said.

"Uh, sir, I don't even think I know your girlfriend, but—"

13

"Not my girlfriend," the man corrected him, "my girl, the one who works for me."

"Oh, you mean . . ." Clint groped for her name and found it. "You mean Raquel."

"Course I mean Raquel."

"I'm sorry," said Clint, who still had Elizabeth on his mind, not Raquel, "how did I insult her?"

"She offered to come to your room for a dollar and you refused," the man said. "What, is a dollar too much?"

"No, no, a dollar is fine—"

"Then what, is she too ugly?"

"No, she's a beautiful girl—"

"She makes extra money bein' a whore," the man said. "Why'd you wanna take that away from her?"

"Look," Clint said, "the problem is she's too . . . young."

"Young? Whataya talkin' about? She's fifteen. She's prime."

Fifteen, Clint thought. Even younger that he had surmised.

"She's not quite . . . developed yet," Clint said. "I tend to like . . . older women . . . larger women . . ."

"Oh," the bartender said, as if it finally dawned on him, "you like fat whores. I can get you a fat whore—"

"No, not fat—"

"Big, then," the man said. "You want a big woman. I can find one of them, too, but bigger is gonna cost more—two dollars!"

"Look," Clint said, harshly, "I don't want one of your whores. Is that clear enough?"

The big man took a step back, as if Clint had struck him across the face.

"What, our whores ain't good enough for you?"

"Jesus . . ." Clint said, at a loss as to what to say next to get the man to leave him alone.

"Hey, boys," the man shouted, "this feller says that Gonzales whores ain't good enough for him."

"I didn't say that—"

Clint was interrupted by the sound of chairs sliding across the floor as the other men in the place stood up. He looked around and found a dozen men scowling at him the way the bartender had been, and these men were armed.

Apparently, the men of Gonzales, Texas, took great pride in their whores.

FIVE

"Now, hold on," Clint said. "I never said your whores weren't good enough."

"Then what are you sayin', señor?" one of the other man asked.

"All I'm saying," Clint tried to explain, "is that I am not a man who uses whores."

"No whores?" the bartender asked, frowning now instead of scowling.

"Here," someone said, and suddenly a boy of about sixteen or so was thrust forward from the crowd of a dozen men. "Maybe he prefers boys."

"*Sí*," another man said, "let him have Pablo!"

They all began to laugh and, red faced, the boy turned and ran back into the crowd of men.

Clint let them have their laugh and waited for it to die down before he spoke again.

"You know," he said, directing his remarks to the bartender, "your food is very good. Did you make it?"

"What?" The bartender looked confused by the ques-

17

tion. "No, I didn't make it. The cook, Raquel's mother, she made it."

"But you own the place, right?"

"Well, yeah, right."

"Then I have to compliment you on your food," Clint said. "And your beer."

"I . . . you . . . uh, thanks, but . . . what about Raquel?"

"Yeah," one of the other men asked, "what about Raquel?"

"Or Pablo," somebody said, and someone else snickered.

"Look," Clint said, "Raquel's lovely, but she's really too good for the likes of me."

"What is happening here?"

It was a new voice, and it was coming from the front door. It was at once frail, but strong. All of the men in the place turned to look, and they all fell silent. Clint had to lean forward to see who the spokesman was. He saw an older man, dressed very well, with a black gaucho-style hat, and standing next to him was Elizabeth Vargas, still dressed like a man, but with a shirt of deep purple. He assumed that the old gentleman with her was her father.

"Don Carlos," the bartender said. "We were just havin' some trouble with a stranger—"

"This gentleman is Clint Adams," Don Carlos Vargas said, "and he is my guest in town."

All eyes now went to Clint, and the bartender repeated, "Clint Adams?"

Someone in the crowd asked, "The Gunsmith?"

"That is correct," Elizabeth said. "The Gunsmith."

Most of the men moved toward the door, slowly at first, then more quickly. Vargas and Elizabeth moved aside to allow them to leave. A braver few simply returned to their tables, and kept their eyes averted from Clint.

The bartender looked at Clint and said, "Sorry, Mr. Adams. Uh, another beer?"

"Three, I think," Clint said. He looked at Elizabeth, who nodded. "Yes, three."

"Yes, sir."

Don Carlos and his daughter moved across the floor to join Clint at his table.

"Clint Adams," Elizabeth said, "may I present my father, Don Carlos Miguel—"

"Not the entire name, please, *mi hija*," Vargas said, raising one hand. "I am sure Mr. Adams does not wish to hear the entire name. Sir, may we sit with you?"

"Please," Clint said, and he stood to hold Elizabeth's chair for her.

"Gracias," she said.

The old man had once been very tall, but now he was slightly bent, costing him an inch or two of his youthful height. He seated himself, and close up, Clint could see that his skin looked like parchment, dotted here and there with brown blemishes. His eyes, though, retained their brightness. The man's body may have been betraying him, but his mind was as sharp as ever.

The bartender returned with the three mugs of beer and set them down on the table.

"Nice to see you again, Don Carlos," the man said, stealing a glance at Elizabeth but not speaking to her.

"You may return to the bar, Arthur."

"Yes, sir."

"What was the trouble when we entered?" Elizabeth asked Clint.

"Um, the bartender—Arthur, is it?—he was upset that I had turned down his, uh, an offer from his girl . . . Raquel."

"You rejected Raquel?" Elizabeth asked, looking amused.

"I'm afraid I did."

"She is very lovely."

"I suppose she is," Clint said, "but she is also very young."

"At my age," Don Carlos said, "everyone is very young, but I understand what you mean."

"I didn't mean any offense," Clint said.

"Do not worry," Don Carlos said. "I will make sure there are no reprisals."

"You can do that?" Clint asked.

"My father," Elizabeth said, "owns the cantina. Arthur and Raquel, and Maria—Raquel's mother—work for him."

"You will not be charged for food or drink while you are in Gonzales," Don Carlos assured Clint, "but may we get down to business now, Señor Adams?"

"That's exactly what I'd prefer to do, sir."

SIX

"I saw him die dead," Don Carlos said, "with my own eyes. A ball hit him right here." The old man touched his forehead above the right eye.

Clint had listened in fascination while Don Carlos described his role at the Alamo. He was a soldier, he said, just a soldier, one of many. Eventually, he said, Santa Anna's superior numbers just overwhelmed the undermanned Americans.

"Are you sure," Clint asked, when the man had finished his tale, "are you sure it was Travis's body you saw?"

"Some of his own men identified him," Don Carlos said, "before they were executed."

"Well," Clint said, with a shrug, "They could have lied."

"They could have," the older man agreed, "but Santa Anna himself identified the body."

"And he knew what Travis looked like?"

"Apparently," Don Carlos said. "He told us he did, and we had no reason to disbelieve him."

"But now?"

"But now . . . I do not know. This man in Goliad . . . this

21

ghost . . . he claims to be Travis." Don Carlos leaned forward and stared intently at Clint. "Señor Adams, I need to know if it is him. And if it is, how did he survive?"

"If it is him," Clint said, "that's a question a lot of us will want answered."

The old man sat back in his chair, looking exhausted.

"Papa—"

"It is nothing," he told his daughter. "I am fine."

"Don Carlos," Clint said, "are there others who, like you, saw Travis dead? Other survivors?"

"If there are some of my comrades still living, I do not know where they are," Vargas said. "I was a young man at the Alamo, and now I am old."

Clint realized that he might very well be looking at the last living survivor of the Alamo. Of course, that was assuming that the man claiming to be William Travis was a fraud.

"Okay," he said.

Both Don Carlos and Elizabeth looked at him.

"Señor?" Vargas said.

"Okay," Clint said, "I'll do it."

Elizabeth grabbed her father's arm anxiously, then leaned over and whispered something into his ear.

"My daughter tells me you were concerned about being compensated for your time—"

"That's not a concern, Don Carlos," Clint assured him.

"I would like to pay your expenses, at the very least," the old man said. "I did not ever expect you to do this for nothing, Señor Adams. You are, after all, a very busy man."

"Not so busy, Don Carlos," Clint said. "Not so busy, at all."

"Then perhaps another drink, to seal the bargain?" Don Carlos asked.

"Yes," Clint said, "definitely another drink."

• • •

Over the drink they discussed the task in more detail.

"You would, of course, have to go to Goliad," the old man said. "My daughter and I are known there, so we may not accompany you."

"This Travis," Elizabeth said, "he has a ranch outside of town. It is heavily guarded, almost like a fortress."

"Almost like the Alamo?"

"Indeed," Don Carlos said. "I had not thought of that before, but that is exactly it."

"How would I get word to you after I've seen this Travis?" Clint asked them.

"There will be someone in Goliad you can talk to," Vargas said. "Someone who can bring us a message."

"Will you be back at your home in Mexico?"

"My hacienda is too far," Don Carlos said. "We will be somewhere between here and Goliad. When we receive word from you, we will ride into Goliad to meet you."

"Don Carlos, forgive me for asking," Clint said, "but once you know the truth, what do you intend to do?"

The older man stared at Clint for a few moments, then said, "I just need to know, señor. I have spent all these years thinking one thing. When you have spent so many years believing a thing . . ."

"I understand," Clint said.

"*Bueno,*" Don Carlos said. "And now I am tired. I must rest."

"Father—" Elizabeth said, helping the old man to his feet.

"No," he said, "I will be fine. Stay, talk with Señor Adams some more." He looked at Clint. "She spends so much time with me, señor. She never gets to talk with anyone her own age."

"Father—"

"Stay, my child," Don Carlos told her. "Stay."

The old man left, not by the front door, but by a door at the back of the cantina.

"Is he going to the hotel?" Clint asked.

"No," she said. "We have somewhere else to stay."

"I've already eaten," Clint said to Elizabeth, "but are you hungry?"

"I am," she said, looking boldly into his eyes, "but not for food. When we were in Labyrinth that night, I wanted you to stay with me."

"I was a gentleman," he said.

"I know," she replied, "but you don't have to be a gentleman again, do you?"

She smiled, and he said, "No, I think I can avoid that mistake again."

She stood, took his hand and led him out the front door and in the direction of the hotel.

SEVEN

Cal Davis entered what he referred to as "the Big House" without knocking and made his way to the room his boss used as an office. Seated behind a large oak desk was a man in his seventies, his head tilted down, his chin on his chest—or where his chest would have been were it not so sunken with age now. He had definitely fallen asleep while doing some paperwork. Davis closed the door quickly behind him and moved to the desk.

"Sir?"

The older man did not stir.

"Mr. Travis?"

He considered touching the man on the shoulder, but the last time he'd done that, he could have sworn his boss was going to have a heart attack. So he just continued to call the man's name out until he finally lifted his chin and opened his eyes.

"Cal?"

"Yes, sir."

The older man sat up suddenly and cleared his throat.

"I was just, uh, resting my eyes."

"Yes, sir."

"What can I do for you?"

"I have some information on Don Carlos, sir."

"That old reprobate? Where is he now? What kind of trouble is he causing?"

"Well, we're not sure, sir," Davis said. "He's left Mexico and has come into Texas."

"Where?"

"Well, our best guess would be Gonzales."

"Gonzales," Travis said. "Hmm, could be headed here, then."

"He could have stopped here first, if this was where he wanted to come," Davis pointed out. Goliad was closer to the border than Gonzales was.

"That's true."

"What should we do, sir?"

"Hmm . . ." The elder stared out into space for a few moments.

"We, uh, could send someone to Gonzales to check it out," Davis offered.

"Yes, yes," the old man said, "let's do that."

"And also have a man in Goliad to keep watch in case he shows up?"

"Yes, excellent idea, lad," the man behind the desk said.

"And, sir, did you sign those papers I gave you?"

"Papers?"

"Yeah, those ranch papers . . . right here." Davis reached over and touched the papers in question. "You were going to review them and sign them."

"Oh, yes, of course." Travis grabbed his quill, dipped it in ink and hastily scrawled his name across the bottom of several sheets of paper. "There."

"Thank you, sir."

"Anything else, Cal?"

"No, sir," Davis said. "That would be it."

"Splendid."

Davis studied the man for a few moments. The old man's eyes were still a bit fuzzy from sleep, and there had been a distinct tremble in his hand when he'd signed. The puckered scar above his left eye stood out starkly against his pale skin. Oddly, he retained all of his hair and, if anything, probably wore it longer now than he had when he was younger. He resembled a lion—an old, tired, worn out lion.

"Cal?"

This time it was the younger man who was prodded from reverie.

"Sorry, sir," he said. "Just thinkin' if there was anythin' else, after all."

"And?"

"No, sir," Davis said. "That's it."

"I'll see you at dinner, then."

"Yes, sir."

Davis left the office, leaving the door open behind him.

Outside, Lex Jackson asked, "Did he sign the papers?"

"He signed 'em."

"Good. Lemme have them."

Davis hesitated.

"You still want me to go to Goliad and file them right?" Jackson asked.

"Yeah, Lex, I do," Davis said, and handed them over. "I also want you to stay in Goliad for a while."

"That won't be no hardship," Jackson said, "but why?"

"Keep an eye out for old Don Carlos," Davis said. "He might show up there."

"Jeez, we still worried about that ol' boy?"

"He could cause some trouble."

"By provin' that the old man ain't the real William Travis, after all?" Jackson asked. "Come on, Cal, do you even believe that?"

"Hey," Davis said, prodding the other man hard with two fingers, "that old man is a hero of the Alamo, whether you believe it or not."

"Okay, okay," Jackson said, backing off, "he's a hero. Whatever you say."

"Just get those papers filed."

"Say," Jackson asked, "what do you think that hero of the Alamo would say if he knew we was stealin' his ranch and holding little by little?"

"He'd probably tell me to kill you," Davis answered, "and do you know what? I just might."

"Hey, hey," Jackson said, "I'm just kiddin', Cal, just kiddin'."

"Yeah," Davis muttered as Jackson turned and headed for the barn, "just kiddin'."

EIGHT

Clint closed the door and turned to face Elizabeth Vargas. She smiled and began to unbutton her shirt.

"No." He stepped forward and stopped her. "I want to do that slowly."

She dropped here hands to her sides. He started with her gunbelt, removing it and letting it drop to the floor. Then he undid the buttons of her shirt, one at a time, slowly bringing her bare flesh into view. She squirmed beneath his touch as he continued to undress her. By the time she was naked, she was covered with goose bumps, and the nipples of her large, heavy breasts were hard.

He held her breasts in the palms of his hands, rubbing her nipples with his thumbs. She pressed her crotch to his, and he could feel the heat of her body through his clothes.

"My turn," she whispered, undoing his gunbelt and letting it drop to the floor with hers. Soon his clothing and hers were in a combined heap on the floor and they had moved to the bed.

Her body fascinated him. The scent that filled his nostrils made him dizzy. Beneath his tongue and fingertips her flesh felt smooth and soft. When she touched him, it felt as if heat was coming from her fingers. As his penis swelled in her hands, he feared their combined heat would start a blaze that would take down the entire building.

He rolled her onto her back and mounted her, teasing her by just touching the tip of his hard cock to her wetness, entering just a bit before pulling out again. She gasped and clutched at him, begged him to slide fully into her, but he wasn't ready. Instead, he kissed his way down her body until her could slide his tongue in and out of her, tasting the tartness of her juices as she wet his cheeks and chin with it. He slid his hands beneath her to clutch her buttocks and press his face to her, as if he was trying to burrow into her. She gasped and cried out as the tip of his tongue found her rigid clit, teasing it, rolling it, loving it. When her time came, she cried out lustily, her nails raking his flesh, grabbing him and pulling him up on top of her so he could enter her. Before the last waves of her first orgasm faded away, he rode her to her second. She bucked beneath him, beating on the bed with her fists and her heels and biting his shoulder to keep from screaming . . .

Later he woke to find her pressed against him from behind, her hands roaming over him, rubbing his butt, kissing the back of his neck and his shoulders. She slid one hand around to the front and began to stroke him. When he was fully erect, she rolled him onto his back, slithered down between his legs and began to kiss and lick him. He groaned when she took him fully into her mouth and began riding him, wetting him, sliding up and down his length while she braced herself with her palms pressed to his thighs. He felt the rush building up in his legs, but he didn't want it to end yet. He grabbed her, pulled her atop him so he could reach her breasts with his mouth. He sucked her nipples into his mouth one at a time, then squeezed her breasts together so he could get both distended nubs into his mouth at one time. She lifted her hips and reached between to guide herself onto him. She groaned as she sat down on him, taking his length fully into her. Just as with their earlier coupling, neither of them said a word. Aside from her sighs and moans, she was possibly the quietest woman he'd ever had sex with, except for right at the end, when she'd let loose with that lusty cry—that is, if she wasn't taking a piece out of his shoulder with her teeth.

She began to bounce up and down on him, her eyes squeezed tightly shut, biting her lower lip, her hair a wild mass of curls cascading down around her bare shoulders. This time when the rush inside of him started to build, he let it, first waiting for it, then moving his hips urgently, chasing it . . .

When he woke next, daylight was streaming in through the window, a shaft of it falling across her bare butt as she slept on her stomach. In that beam of morning light her ass looked majestic, and first he ran his hands over it, enjoying the feel of each orb, then leaned down to run his tongue along the cleft between them. She groaned and wriggled her butt as he slid a hand beneath her to cup her vagina and then slide one finger up and down, getting her wet. She tried to turn over but he stopped her. Instead, he pulled her up onto all fours and positioned himself behind her. Despite the fact they'd had sex several times already that night, his penis was as hard or harder than it had ever been. He slid it between her warm thighs and up into her heat, then held her hips as he moved in and out of her, slowly at first, then increasing the speed until the air filled with the sound of their flesh slapping together. At one point, he reached for her beautiful hair, wrapped it in his hand and pulled back so that her neck was stretched. Her breath began to come in gasps and he felt her behind shudder as her time approached. He did his best to go with her, but she got there first, burying her face in the pillow to muffle her screams, and then he exploded inside of her and collapsed with his weight on top of her, both of them at once laughing and gasping for air.

"You are going to kill me," she said.

"Not if you kill me first."

"I have never known a man such as you," she said some time later, while they were laying side by side in bed together.

"A man like what?"

"So . . . so vibrant," she said. "So much energy. Frankly, I have never been with a man who could match me, who was as . . . hungry as I am, do you know?"

"I think you're just getting the last of it," he said. "This is my final surge of energy before I become a withered old man."

She slid her hand down between his legs and fondled him. Immediately, he began to stir to her touch.

"Not so withered," she said.

He reached down and slapped her hand away. "Stop it. I'm hungry."

"So am I," she said.

"I meant for food."

She laughed, bit his shoulder and removed her hand. "Actually, so did I."

"Let's get dressed and go find some breakfast."

"And my father," she said, sitting up in bed.

"Oh? Why?"

"You must give him your final answer."

"Have I made up my mind?"

She looked at him over her shoulder, and she was incredibly beautiful, even with her hair almost a rat's nest of tangles after the night they'd had together.

"I think perhaps you have," she said.

He hesitated a moment, then said, "I think I have, too."

NINE

If Don Carlos Vargas had any inkling about what his daughter and Clint Adams had been doing all night, he gave no indication. They had breakfast together in a small cantina—smaller than the one they had been in the night before. Clint wondered idly if Don Carlos owned this one, as well.

The waitress in this one was a middle-aged woman with thick hips and hair on her upper lip.

"*Gracias,* Lupe," Don Carlos said as she laid their breakfast down in front of them.

"Tell me about the law in Goliad," Clint said.

"The sheriff's name is Strode . . ." Don Carlos trailed off and looked at his daughter.

"Andy," she said, "Andy Strode." She looked at Clint. "He works for the man who calls himself Travis. He and his deputies."

"How many deputies?"

"Two, the last time I was there," she said. "That was about two weeks ago."

"Does Travis know you?" Clint asked. "Both of you?"

35

"I have never spoken to him," Don Carlos said, "or seen him."

Clint looked at Elizabeth.

"I have seen him," she said, "but he does not know who I am."

"Who else does he have working for him?"

"He has a ranch, with many hands," she said.

"What about his foreman?"

"His name is Cal Davis. He was with Travis when he first came to Goliad," Elizabeth explained. "He did all the hiring."

"How many hands?"

She shrugged. "A dozen or so, I think. It's not a big spread, but it's growing."

"He is as old as I am," Vargas said. "He does not have time to build it slowly."

"What do the people of Goliad think of him?"

"They are split," Elizabeth said. "Some revere him as a hero, some fear him . . . They call him the Ghost of Goliad."

"Elizabeth," Clint asked, "Cal Davis and his men, are they ranch hands, or gunhands?"

"A little bit of both, I think. They walk around town like they own it, and when they want something they do not pay for it, ever."

"And the townspeople go along with that?"

"They do not have much choice," Elizabeth said. "Davis and his men are in control."

"When will you go?" Don Carlos asked.

"Today," Clint said. "Right after breakfast."

"There is a man in Goliad who will meet you," Vargas said. "He will keep us in contact."

"What's his name?"

"Eddie Guerrero," Vargas said.

"He is my cousin," Elizabeth added. "He is a good man. He will help you."

"All right," Clint said. "Why don't we stop talking and eat, and then I can be on my way."

"I am very grateful, Señor Adams."

"Let's wait and see what I find out, Don Carlos," Clint said, "and then you can be grateful."

After breakfast Clint went to saddle Eclipse, leaving Don Carlos and his daughter alone to talk.

"You did well, my daughter."

"He was not hard to convince, Papa."

"Not for you, perhaps," the old man said. "Now that we have him on our side, are you prepared to do what must be done?"

"Sí, Papa," she said. "I have always been prepared."

"You are a good daughter."

But, she thought to herself, I am a better son.

When Clint came walking out of the livery leading his big Darley Arabian, Elizabeth was waiting there.

"Where's your father?" he asked.

"I wanted to say goodbye to you alone."

"Right here, in broad daylight?"

She laughed. "I do not intend to do anything I could not do in broad daylight."

"That's too bad."

"This is a beautiful animal," she said, looking past him at Eclipse.

"Yes, he is."

She turned serious.

"You will have to be very careful in Goliad," she said. "Once Cal Davis and his men know that you are asking about the man who calls himself Travis, you will be in danger."

"Then I'll have to take steps to see that they don't hear about it," Clint said.

"How will you do that?"

"I don't know," he said. "I'll have to wait until I get there and have a look around."

"If you tell Eddie you need me," she said, touching his arm, "I will be there."

"I'll keep that in mind," he said.

She gave him a hug and he mounted up.

"For my father," she said, looking up at him, "I say thank you."

"And like I told him," he replied, "let's wait to see what I can do before you thank me."

"*Vaya con Dios*," she said.

"I hope so."

TEN

Clint decided to make one extra stop before going to Goliad. He was too close to the Alamo now not to stop and at least have a look.

When it came into view—the fort, the mission, whatever people called it—he stopped and viewed it from a distance, first. He wondered if he was standing right where Santa Anna might have stood, planning his attack. Even if only a small part of the story was true—two hundred Americans holding off thirteen hundred Mexicans—it was still an amazing feat on their part.

He rode closer so he could clearly see the walls. Some of them had crumbled, some still stood. The blood of the dead had long ago been absorbed into the ground, but for some reason he did not feel like dismounting. There was no reason to go inside, where so many had been slaughtered and died. According to some Indian legends, the spirits of the dead—some of them, anyway—would still be there, trapped, and he had no desire to walk among them. All he had wanted to do was ride by and take a look, and he had done that.

Now he turned Eclipse and headed for Goliad, where one spirit in particular might still be walking.

As he rode into town, he immediately saw the difference between it and Gonzales. Goliad was alive with activity, had more obviously thriving businesses and was still growing. This was made obvious by the appearance of several new buildings along the main street.

Clint had to go through the amenities first, everything you had to do when you rode into town—the livery, the hotel. There were times when he'd check in with the local law, as well, to let them know he was there, but not this time. He wanted to keep that quiet, for the moment.

He took a room in a small, old hotel rather than the newer one. Leaving behind his saddlebags and rifle, he took to the street to have a look around. He wanted to get the lay of the land before he even stopped in one of the saloons to have a drink.

By the time he'd walked the whole town, he had built up a fierce thirst. From all appearances Goliad was a thriving town. The people seemed peaceful and friendly, many of them nodding to him or bidding him a good day. It did not have the appearance of a town that was under the thumb of one man, or a band of men. He'd seen towns like that before, had seen the fear in the eyes of their people when he, a stranger, walked by them. There was none of that here.

As with Gonzales, Goliad seemed to have an equal number of Mexican and American citizens. The same went for their business establishments. He saw a Chico's Café and a Blue Plate Restaurant. He also saw an equal number of cantinas and saloons. He decided to have a beer first in a saloon, and then in one of the cantinas.

He chose a busy looking saloon with a sign above the door that said "ANDERSON'S." Inside he saw no frills, just a long, scarred oak bar, worn tables and chairs, no stage, no gambling paraphernalia, no girls working the floor—but it might have been too early for that. In one corner was a piano, but it was covered with a layer of dust.

The bartender was waiting for him we he got to the bar. He had a pleasant, red face, clear, bright blue eyes and light brown hair, appeared to be in his thirties.

"Help ya?"

"Beer."

"Comin' up, friend."

The bartender drew a cold one and set it down in front of Clint.

"Passin' through?" he asked.

"Pretty much."

"On your way to where?"

"Nowhere in particular," Clint said. "Just riding."

"Driftin', huh?"

"Yep."

The barman put his elbows on the bar.

"Sometimes I think about sellin' this place, getting' me a horse and driftin' around."

"Why don't you do it?"

"No nerve, I guess," the man said, "but I'm getting' closer to givin' it a try."

"Oh? Why's that?"

The bartender seemed to think before speaking, then said, "Oh, just getting' fed up with the shit, I guess."

"What kind of—"

"Sorry," the man said, "I got another customer."

The man moved off down the bar. Clint assumed he was the namesake of the place, Anderson. He sounded like a man who was being pushed too far. Clint filed away his name as someone to talk to at length at a later time.

He nursed his beer and checked out the other men in the

place. Several at the bar, a few others seated—they all looked as if their minds were not occupied with anything other then the drink in front of them. There wasn't much in the way of conversation going on, and that was the only indication that things might not be right in that town. Men in a saloon usually had a lot to say over a whiskey or a beer. These men were oddly silent.

When he got to the bottom of his mug the bartender came back.

"Another?"

"No, thanks," Clint said. "This place is too quiet for me, more like a . . . an undertaker's than a saloon."

"You won't find it much different in other places," the bartender said, "but you're welcome to try."

"You Anderson?"

"That's me."

Clint dropped a coin on the bar and said, "Thanks very much for the beer."

"You stayin' in town long?"

"I don't know," Clint said. "Any reason I shouldn't?"

"Any reason you should?"

Suddenly, Clint saw something else in the man's face, something lurking behind the good-natured smile, the easy manner.

"There something you're trying to tell me, friend?"

"Me?" Anderson asked. "I'm just a saloon owner, a bartender. I got nothin' to say that anybody wants to hear."

"You never know," Clint said. "I might want to hear it."

Anderson tossed a towel up onto his shoulder and said, "I got work to do, mister. You take a look at the other places in town, and when you want another cold beer, you come on back."

"I'll do that, Mr. Anderson," Clint said. "I'll do that."

ELEVEN

Clint's next stop was a small cantina with no name showing anywhere. On the wall next to the door someone had scrawled the word "Cantina," but that was it.

He went inside. If Anderson's was no frills, this place was even less. The bar was made of odd pieces of wood and, right in the center, a wooden door. Some of the tables had three legs instead of four. Here, however, there were two dark-haired, black-eyed, olive-skinned Mexican girls working the floor. They didn't have much work to do, though, since there was only three other men in the place, not counting the sweaty, overweight bartender.

"What can I get you, señor?" the bartender asked. Clint caught the glint of several gold teeth.

"What's good?"

"*Cerveza, señor,*" the man said, "unless you have a death wish."

"What are my choices then?"

The man shrugged. "Rotgut whiskey, some mescal or tequila."

"I'll take the beer."

"A wise choice."

The bartender filled a mug with beer and brought it to Clint, who found it lukewarm, at best. There was also a dead fly floating on top. He picked it out and flicked it away without a word.

The general attitude in this place seemed to mirror that of Anderson's. None of the men were talking; the two girls were standing at the other end of the bar, looking bored. Clint decided to engage them in some conversation to see what it would yield.

"Ladies," he said, moving to their end of the bar.

Up close he realized that they could have been sisters—younger and older—or they could even have been mother and daughter. The younger one appeared to be in her twenties, fresh-faced where the other woman seemed a bit world-weary, as if she'd been standing at the end of that bar for years. She could have been anywhere from mid-thirties to mid-forties, but both women were lovely, had the same body type, busty and long-legged, the older one perhaps a bit thicker in the waist.

"Señor," the older one said.

"Will this place liven up later on this evening?"

"Perhaps," the younger said, giving him a flirtatious look. "What did you have in mind?"

"Maybe just some conversation," Clint said.

"Talk is all you want, señor?" the older woman asked.

"It would be a start," Clint said. He stepped back to eye them critically. "You two must be sisters."

"*Sí, señor,*" the older woman said, "we are sisters." Her tone said, *We'll be whatever you want us to be.*

"Perhaps you would be interested in something more than conversation?" the young woman asked. "My . . . sister and I are not very busy now, as you can see."

"I do see," Clint said. "I've only just arrived in this town, but it seems pretty quiet, almost sleepy."

"That could change, señor," the young woman said, "in the blink of an eye."

"Carmen!" the older woman said, quickly. *"Silencio."*

Carmen looked properly chastised.

"We must go to work, señor," the older woman said, "unless there is something you want from us now?"

"No, ladies," Clint said, "nothing now. I was just looking to pass the time."

"If you wish to pass the time later—" Carmen said, running her finger along the soft flesh of her bosom.

She was cut off as the older woman grabbed her arm and said, "Carmen! Come!" and pulled her away.

Clint turned to return to his place at the bar, and found himself the object of the attention of the other four men. The looks on their faces were ones of boredom, though, so he didn't feel he had attracted any unwanted attention, yet.

He finished his beer, said to the bartender, "Thanks," and left the cantina.

TWELVE

After he'd been in town for a few hours, Clint began to detect the undercurrent. This time when men nodded to him and women greeted him on the street, he saw that there was something there other than just goodwill. In a town where sides had most likely been drawn, they didn't know which side he was on, so they had to be careful.

The smell hit him before he saw the place, and his stomach immediately started growling. It was a tiny café, but there were big smells coming from it, and he followed them right to the door.

Like both of the drinking establishments he'd been in, this café was small. The tables and chairs, however, seemed to have been lovingly handmade by someone who cared what their place of business looked like.

"Ah, señor," a man said, coming out of the kitchen. "Welcome to my humble restaurant."

He was a big man with an apron that was covering him almost from head to toe. There were stains on it, but they were indications that he spent much of his time in the kitchen, and did not put Clint off, at all. Especially considering the wonderful smells coming from that kitchen.

"I couldn't pass it up," Clint said. "It smells so good in here. You're the owner?"

"The owner," the man said, "the cook, the waiter, the swamper . . . it is my place and I do everything. Would you like a table?"

"Yes, I would."

The man looked him up and down and Clint saw his eyes pause on his gun.

"A table against the wall, perhaps?"

"That would be fine."

"This way, please."

This was a man who was not wearing a mask to hide his real feelings. Clint felt that he was genuinely as happy as he seemed to be.

"Señor, my name is Pedro Bejarano and it is my pleasure to serve you," the man said. "What would you like?"

"What's good, Pedro?"

"Señor," the man said, "that is like asking me which of my eight children is the best." He spread his arms expansively. "Everything I cook is good."

"Steak?"

"Just a steak?" Pedro asked, looking disappointed. "I can do many things with steak, señor."

"I tell you what," Clint said, "I'll put myself in your hands. You have a hungry man, here. Feed me."

"Excellent, señor," Pedro said, "excellent, leave everything to me. You are my only customer at the moment, so you will have my undivided attention."

True to his word, Clint had all of Pedro's attention, and the man fed him very well. Enchiladas with the most tender of steak inside, along with some vegetables done to perfection and rolled up inside with the meat, and then some beans and rice alongside it. Clint had had enchiladas before, but there was something special about the sauce Pedro prepared. It was the best Mexican meal he'd ever had, and when he was finished he told the man so.

"Gracias, señor," Pedro said. "It always does my heart good to feed a man well and have him appreciate it."

"Well, I do appreciate it, Pedro," Clint said. "It makes me wonder why every table in this place isn't full."

"Oh, that," Pedro said. "I'm afraid that is because of Mr. Travis and his men.".

"Travis?"

Pedro sat down opposite Clint, who thought he was about to get some valuable information without ever having asked for it.

"He would like people to think that he is William Travis—you know, the one who was killed at the Alamo?"

"Yes, I know who William Travis is," Clint said. "But all of the Americans at the Alamo died."

"This man has half the town convinced that he is Travis, and he did not die at the hands of Santa Anna."

"And what's that got to do with you having no customers?"

"His foreman is Cal Davis, and he has let all the townspeople know that they should not eat here."

"And why is that?"

"Because I don't believe Travis is who he says he is," Pedro said, "and because I had the nerve to expect his men to pay me when they eat here."

"They don't pay other places?"

"Most of the others in town have agreed to feed them, or give them what they want, for nothing," Pedro said. "That is not the way for a man to make a living, señor. Am I not right?"

"I think you are very right," Clint said. "Tell me, Pedro, have you ever seen this Travis?"

"One time," the man answered. "He's very old, and has a scar here." Pedro touched his forehead. "That is where William Travis was supposed to have been hit by a ball fired from a Mexican gun. Shot through the forehead and killed."

"That would be quite a wound for a man to survive."

"Yes," Pedro said, "it would, but this man has many convinced. They even call him the Ghost of Goliad."

"That's odd."

"What is?"

Clint said, "I'd think they'd call him the Ghost of the Alamo."

THIRTEEN

Pedro was the first person Clint asked specific questions of.

"How often do Travis's men come into town?"

"Several times a week," the café owner said. "There is no telling when they will appear."

"And when they do? They have the town under their thumb?" Clint asked.

"Yes, they do," Pedro said, "and they enjoy it. They take what they want . . . clothes, food, women—"

"They rape women?" Clint asked. If the town put up with that, he'd be surprised.

"It is not rape," Pedro said. "So far the women they have chosen have gone with them willingly."

"But what will happen the first time a woman resists?" Clint wondered aloud.

"I do not know," Pedro said, with a fatalistic shrug. "I suppose we will find out."

"What about Travis?" Clint asked. "Does he ever come to town?"

"He has been to town, but does not make a habit of it," Pedro said. "I believe I have only seen him twice in a year."

"Does anyone ever go out to see him?"

"No one really gets to talk to him," Pedro said. "Cal Davis is more than just his foreman, he is his voice."

"What about a sheriff?" Clint asked. He didn't want to let on that he already knew the answer.

"Andy Strode," Pedro said. "He was hired by Travis, and he answers to Davis."

"Does he do his job?"

"He does it very well," Pedro said, "as long as it does not interfere with any of Travis's men."

"And his deputies?" Clint asked. "Do they get what they want the way Travis's men do?"

"No," Pedro said, "they do not enjoy the same benefits as the men who work for Travis."

Clint finished the last of his food and pushed the plate away.

"Some more?" Pedro asked.

"God, no," Clint said, touching his belly. "Two helpings is more than enough. I'm full."

"And satisfied?"

"Very."

"Bueno," Pedro said, happily. He got to his feet and collected the empty plate. "More coffee?"

"One more cup," Clint said. "I think that's all I can handle."

"I will bring it."

Pedro disappeared into the kitchen, and as he did a man appeared in the doorway. He was Mexican, and young, in his twenties. He had a worn gunbelt around his waist, and a handgun with an equally worn grip. He looked both ways before entering.

"Señor Adams?" he asked.

"That's right."

"I am Eddie," the man said. "Eddie Guerrero."

"Elizabeth's cousin."

"*Sí.*"

"Have a seat."

"*Gracias.*"

As Eddie sat, Pedro came out of the kitchen with a cup of fresh coffee. He scowled at Eddie as he set it down.

"What are you doing here?"

"Relax, *viejo,*" Eddie said. "I am here to speak with Señor Adams."

"Do not bother my customers."

"What customers?" Guerrero asked, with a laugh. "I don't see any customers."

"It's okay, Pedro," Clint said.

"Is he a friend of yours?" Pedro asked.

"Not a friend," Clint said. "We've just met, but I want to talk to him. Why don't you bring Eddie a cup of coffee?"

"I will, but only because you have asked," Pedro said, then looked at Eddie and added, "And don't call me 'old man.'"

Eddie laughed as Pedro went back to the kitchen.

"What's the problem between you and Pedro?" Clint asked.

"There is no problem," Eddie said. "It is a game that we play, that is all. Do not concern yourself."

"Fine," Clint said. "Where have you been? I've been in town all day."

"I know," Eddie said, "I have seen you."

"You've been following me?"

"I have," Eddie said. "Is that bad?"

"No." What was bad was that Clint had never spotted him. Either he was getting careless, or Eddie was really good at what he did.

Pedro came out with Eddie's coffee, set it down and returned to the kitchen.

"How much has Pedro told you?" Eddie asked.

"Quite a bit," Clint said.

"What more do you need to know?"

"I assume you know where the Travis ranch is?"

"Of course."

"Then that's all I need to know, for now," Clint said. "How to get there."

"You will be going out there?"

"Not right away," Clint said, "but eventually."

"I will go with you."

"No," Clint said, "when I go out, I'll go alone. For now, I don't think we should be seen together. As I understand it, your task is to contact Don Carlos when the time comes."

"My task is to help," Eddie said. "I will do that any way that you request, señor."

"Okay, fine," Clint said. "Right now I request that you drink your coffee."

"That is all?"

"That's all," Clint said, "for now."

FOURTEEN

Andy Strode looked up as the door to his office opened and his two deputies stepped in.

"What's going on it town?" he asked.

"Not much," Deputy Steve Collins said. He perched a hip on the second desk in the room, took off his hat and ran his hand through his shock of blond hair. At thirty-five, it was shot through with bits of gray. He'd been a deputy in Goliad for eight months and didn't like the job. But being a deputy was all he knew, and this was his job until something better came along.

"Any of Travis's men in town?"

"No," Terry Madison said. He was ten years younger than Collins, and at least that many years behind him in experience. The only thing he had over Collins was that he'd been a deputy in Goliad for two years. "But there is a stranger in town."

"A stranger?" Strode asked. "Who?"

"I don't know," Madison said.

"Did you check the hotel?"

"Not yet," Collins said. "Next step."

"I'll do it," Strode said, standing up. At forty, he towered over both men physically, standing six-four. He strapped on his gun and walked toward the door. "What hotel?"

"The little one by the livery," Madison said.

"Want some company?" Collins asked.

"No," Strode said. "I'll handle it."

"Fine," the older deputy said, getting up off the desk. "I could use a cup of coffee, anyway."

As Strode left, Collins went to the stove and poured himself a cup of coffee.

"Who do you think the stranger is?" Madison asked.

"No idea," Collins said. "Coffee?"

"Sure."

Sheriff Strode went to the small hotel and presented himself at the desk.

"Sheriff," the clerk said, "what can I do—"

"You got a new guest today."

"Yes, sir—"

"I need a name."

"Uh, I don't know, but it's in the register . . ."

"You didn't look?"

"No, sir," the man said. "I mean . . . he took a room. I didn't need to know—"

Strode turned the register around and opened it. He found the name Clint Adams in it and slammed it shut.

"Uh, do you know him?"

"I know of him."

"Who is—" the clerk started, but the lawman turned and stalked out of the building.

The clerk turned the book around, opened it and located the name for himself.

"Jesus," he said.

• • •

Sheriff Strode stopped just outside the hotel. Where would he be now if he was Clint Adams? Getting a drink? Something to eat? And why would The Gunsmith be in Goliad? Was this something Strode should check out for himself, or pass along to Cal Davis? Well, if he was a real sheriff he'd check it out, but he wasn't, was he? He was Travis's little puppet sheriff—or Cal Davis's.

He decided to take a turn around town and see if he could locate the new visitor. A simple little talk, a few questions, should reveal whether The Gunsmith was in town for a reason, or just passing through.

FIFTEEN

Clint told Eddie Guerrero to leave the café ahead of him.

"But first, how do I get ahold of you in case I need you?" he asked.

"I will be around, Señor Adams," Eddie said, "but if you really want me, leave a message here with Pedro."

"Pedro? I thought he didn't like you?"

Eddie frowned.

"Whatever made you think that?"

Before Clint could comment, Eddie left.

"Pedro!"

The man came running out from the kitchen.

"Let me settle my bill."

"Sí, señor,"

The man told Clint what he owed and he paid it.

"What's going on with you and Eddie?"

"Nothing, señor."

"Are you friends, or what?"

"Uhhhh, friends . . . well, that is a fairly strong word, señor. We are . . . related."

"Related?"

"He is my cousin."

"Then . . . does that make his cousin your cousin?"

"In a Mexican family that is not necessarily true."

"Okay . . . so if I need to get in touch with him, I can
leave a message here with you?"

"*Sí, señor*, but I must warn you . . ."

"About what?"

"Do not let him involve you in any of his schemes."

"I think it's safe to say I'm not involved in any of his
schemes, Pedro," Clint said. "Thanks."

"Come back again, señor," Pedro said. "It is a pleasure
to feed a man who enjoys good food."

"I'll be back."

Clint walked out the door and came face-to-face with a
man wearing a sheriff's badge.

"Clint Adams?"

"That's right."

"I'm Sheriff Andy Strode."

"Nice to meet you, Sheriff."

"Can we go somewhere and talk?" the lawman asked.

"Where did you have in mind, Sheriff?"

"How does my office sound?"

"Why not?" Clint asked. "Lead the way?"

Sheriff Andy Strode opened the door to his office and allowed Clint to precede him. The building was adobe and
had been there a long time. Inside Clint found two desks,
both occupied by deputies, and the ever-present gun racks
on the wall behind one of them. The deputy seated at the
desk in front of the racks leaped to his feet when he saw
the sheriff enter the office.

"Sorry, Sheriff," he said, "I was just—"

"Never mind."

Clint looked at the other deputy, who looked back at him silently and didn't move.

"Boys, why don't you both take a turn around town?" Strode said. "Mr. Adams and I are going to have a talk."

"Adams?" Terry Madison asked.

"Come on, Terry," Steve Collins said, getting to his feet. "Let's take a walk."

"But Adams," Madison said, as Collins led him out the door. "Adams who?"

"If you were supposed to know that," Collins said, pulling the door closed behind them, "the sheriff wold have told you."

"Have a seat, Mr. Adams."

Clint sat in front of the man's desk while the sheriff walked around behind it and seated himself.

"I know who you are," Strode said.

"So?"

"What are you doing in Goliad?"

"Passing through."

"On your way to where?"

"Nowhere in particular," Clint said.

"From where?"

"Same answer."

"So you're just drifting?"

"Pretty much."

"And you're not here for any particular reason?"

"That's right."

"And did you intend to stop in and let me know you were in my town?"

"You know," Clint said, "I was on my way to do just that. By the way, how did you know where to find me?"

"Pedro's has the best food in town. I figured somebody would have steered you there, or you would have followed your nose."

"I followed my nose," Clint confirmed. "He tells me he doesn't have too many customers, lately."

"That's pretty much his own fault."

"Why's that?"

"Local politics," Strode said. "If you're just passing through, you wouldn't be interested, would you?"

"You never know," Clint said. "I find all kinds of things interesting."

"How long do you intend to stay in town, Mr. Adams?" the sheriff asked, changing the subject.

"I don't know, really," Clint said. "I thought I might take advantage of being here and take a look at the Alamo."

"You can do that on the way out of town."

"Thanks for the tip." Clint stood up. "Is there any reason you'd like me to leave town?"

"I just don't want any trouble."

"Neither do I."

"Unfortunately," Strode said, "men like you attract it like . . . well, like corpses attract flies."

"Very visual of you, Sheriff," Clint said. "I'm going to do my best to avoid any kind of trouble while I'm here."

"And, again, that would be how long?"

Clint spread his hands.

"I'm afraid I haven't decided."

"Well, do me a favor, will you?"

"Anything."

"When you do decide, let me know."

SIXTEEN

When Clint left the sheriff's office, he looked up and down the street. There was no sign of the two deputies. He decided to go over to his hotel and just wait. He'd been sitting in a rickety wooden chair for about half an hour when Deputy Steve Collins appeared. The man stepped up onto the boardwalk and leaned against the wall.

"Hello, Clint."

"Steve."

"Never expected to run into you here."

"I never expected to be here," Clint said. "Pull up a chair, if it'll hold you."

"I'll stand. Thanks for not sayin' anything at the office about knowin' me."

"Figured you had your reasons," Clint said.

Collins was one of those men Clint had run into now and then over the years. Sometimes he was behind the badge, and sometimes on the other side. One time he was a bounty hunter and another time a gambler. There was even a time Clint had discovered the man tending bar on a riverboat on the Mississippi.

"What brought you here?" Clint asked.

"Just looking for a quiet place."

"And how'd you come to be wearing the badge?"

"Sheriff needed a deputy," Collins said. "It was either that or go to work for that Travis fella."

"No other choice?"

"I caught on pretty quick that you were either for them or against them. Wearin' the badge is sorta like goin' halfway."

"I see."

"What brings you here?"

"Like I told your boss," Clint said. "Just passing through."

"Why don't I believe that?" Collins asked.

"Don't know."

"Maybe it's because every time I've ever run into you, you were tryin' to help somebody."

"Keeping to my own business these days."

"The business of drifting?"

"That's about it."

Collins studied Clint for a few moments, then shook his head and said, "Not buyin' what you're sellin', Clint."

"You going to give the sheriff that opinion?"

Collins shrugged. "Naw, he forms his own opinions."

"Where's the other deputy?"

"Makin' his rounds."

"Did you tell him you knew me?"

"No. He'd get too excited."

Clint remained silent for a few moments, then thought, what the hell?

"What is this I hear about this fella Travis?" Clint asked.

"What'd you hear?"

"That he claims to be the same Travis that was at the Alamo," Clint said. "That can't be, can it?"

"I dunno," Collins said. "Can it?"

"Have you seen him?"

"Once."

"And?"

"He's an old man," the deputy said. "Sure is old enough to have been at the Alamo, though."

"And what about his men? I hear they've got this town under their thumb."

"That's why I had to figure out a way to stay in this town without picking sides," Collins said.

"So when they come to town, you badge toters stay out of their way?"

"That's the way it works."

"Why would you want to stay in this town under those conditions?" Clint asked.

"I just need a place to hole up," Collins said. "This place has a few saloons, and a couple of good restaurants, a decent white whore and a decent Mexican one."

"All the comforts of home."

"Enough for me."

Clint nodded and fell silent.

"You here to start trouble?" Collins asked, after a few moments.

"I never go anywhere to start trouble, Steve."

"You here to finish some trouble, then?" Collins asked. "Wait a minute . . . Did somebody from this town import you to go against Travis and his boys?"

"I'd be foolish to take a job like that on alone, wouldn't I?" Clint asked.

"Maybe you ain't alone."

"Any other strangers in town?"

"Wouldn't have to be a stranger," Collins said. "There are folks in town who ain't happy about the way things are."

"I can safely say," Clint responded truthfully, "that I'm not working for anybody in town."

SEVENTEEN

By the end of the day, Lex Jackson thought he knew enough about the stranger to ride back to the ranch and tell Cal Davis about him. He'd checked the register in the hotel—the way the sheriff had—and discovered that he was Clint Adams. Naturally, he knew who The Gunsmith was. He'd also seen Adams having a talk with both the sheriff and one of the deputies. But it wasn't his task to check out strangers. Davis wanted to know if Don Carlos Vargas or his daughter had appeared in town.

Jackson knew who Elizabeth Vargas was, and wouldn't have minded if she came to town. She was the best-looking woman he had ever seen in his life.

He decided that just knowing that The Gunsmith was here didn't mean much. The man could have just been passing through. And, of course, since the sheriff worked for Travis, there was an easy enough way to confirm that.

At the moment Jackson was across the street from where Adams and Steve Collins were talking. He decided to head over to the sheriff's office right now and put the question to the man.

• • •

"You know who that fella across the street is?" Clint asked.

"You mean the one watchin' us?"

"That's the one."

"His name's Jackson," Collins said. "He works on the Travis ranch. Well, actually, he works for Cal Davis, Travis's foreman."

"So you refer to the old man as Travis?" Clint asked. "You accept him as William Travis?"

"He says that's his name," Collins replied. "Whether or not he's the Alamo Travis doesn't really matter much to me."

"Jackson's leaving," Clint said. "Any reason he'd ride out and tell his boss I'm here?"

"Only if he thought you were here to go against them," the deputy said, "and you claim you're not, right?"

"Right."

"Then I guess I better get goin'," Collins said. "Young Terry's gonna wonder where I got to."

"It's been good to see you, Steve."

"Yeah," Collins said, "you, too, Clint."

And as he walked away he thought, *So far.*

When the door to the office opened Andy Strode looked up, expecting to see one of his deputies. Instead, it was Cal Davis's right-hand man, Lex Jackson.

"Lex," he said.

"Hello, Andy," Jackson said.

"What can I do for you?"

"I see there's a stranger in town," Jackson said. "Have you checked on him?"

"I have."

"Then you know he's The Gunsmith."

"Yes, I do, Lex," Strode said. "That is my job, remember?"

Jackson sat across from Strode, crossed one leg over a knee and stared at him.

"What's he doin' in town, Andy?"

"Nothing," Strode said. "Just passin' through."

"He says."

"Yes, he does."

"And you believe him?"

"I do."

"So there's nothin' for me to tell Cal?"

"Nothing I can think of, Lex."

Jackson stared at the sheriff a little bit longer, then shrugged and said, "Okay." He stood up and stared for the door, then stopped and turned.

"By the way, did you send either of your deputies to talk to him?"

"No, I didn't. Why?"

"I just saw your man Collins talkin' to Adams in front of his hotel," Jackson said. "I just thought maybe he was followin' orders."

"If he is, they're not mine."

"Okay, then," Jackson said. "I'll be around town for a while, Andy."

"Fine," Strode said.

"Yeah, fine," Jackson said, and walked out.

Strode sat behind his desk for a while, thinking about Clint Adams and Steve Collins. He didn't know much about Collins, except that he seemed to be experienced. He'd hired him for two reasons. First because of his experience, and second because he thought he might have been sent by Cal Davis. Over the course of the eight months he'd decided that Collins was not working for Davis, or for Travis. But what was Collins doing talking to Clint Adams? Was he doing it for the old man, or was he doing it on his own?

Strode stood up, took his gunbelt off a peg on the wall behind him and strapped it on.

EIGHTEEN

Before Steve Collins could locate Terry Madison, Sheriff Andy Strode located Collins. They ran into each other on the street in front of Anderson's saloon.

"Got a minute, Steve?" the sheriff asked.

"You're the boss, Sheriff."

"Let's go into Anderson's," Strode said. "I could use a beer."

Strode led the way to the bar and ordered two beers. A couple of cowboys moved down the bar to give the two lawmen some room. They were not from the Travis ranch, or they would not have moved.

"What's on your mind, Boss?" Collins asked.

"Clint Adams."

"What about him?"

"Do you know him?"

"I saw him in your office—"

"No," Strode said, "I mean, did you know him before he came to town?"

"I met him, once or twice," Collins said.

"Why didn't you tell me that?"

71

Collins shrugged.

"Didn't think it was important," he said, "and he didn't seem to recognize me."

"So you went and reminded him?"

"Hey, I was makin' my rounds and there he was, Sheriff," Collins said. "I just stopped to talk."

"He tell you why he was in town?"

"He didn't tell me anything he didn't tell you," Collins said. "He's just passin' through."

Strode sat back in his chair.

"I want you to stay on him the whole time he's here," he said, finally. "He spits in the street, I want to know about it."

"Okay," Collins said, "but you should know that Lex Jackson was watchin' him."

"I know that Jackson is in town, Steve," Strode said. "I do my job. Just make sure you do yours."

"Yes, sir."

"You know where Terry is?"

"Not exactly," Collins said. "Makin' rounds."

"Find him, tell him that you've got a new assignment. He'll have to make all the rounds himself."

"I'll tell him."

"Then go do it."

Collins nodded and left the office.

Lex Jackson decided to leave watching The Gunsmith to the local law. He had better things to do. He looked down at the bobbing blond head in his lap, leaned his head back and surrendered to the feel of her mouth sliding up and down his cock. The whore had been working most of the day, and the sex smell coming off of her excited him. Her name was Angel, and she was one of two girls he regularly visited at Mabel's Cathouse.

Jackson started to groan as the girl worked him to the

point of an explosion, and then she released him from her mouth and sat back on her heels.

"I wanna ride that big monster," she told him. "Lie back."

"Whatever you say, baby," he muttered, flopping onto his back on the bed.

Angel crawled up on top of him, held him with her hands and slid down onto him.

"Oh, girlllllllll . . . ," he growled, and closed his eyes . . .

"Yeah, that's my big man," Angel cooed, riding him up and down. She leaned over him so that her little tits were hanging in front of his face. He snapped at them with his mouth, but she kept them away from his mouth as she continued to ride his cock.

The girl knew that if she gave Jackson the ride of his life he'd throw her some extra money when they were done, money she didn't have to share with Mabel. She dug her nails into his chest and kept her nipples tantalizingly close to his mouth without letting him get to them. She didn't like when he drooled on her breasts. She knew that the other girl, Ellen, also hated it, and she had big breasts—so big it was hard to keep them away from Jackson's mouth. But you had to say one thing for the man, he was generous.

She watched his face. His eyes were closed, and he was getting redder and redder the closer he got to completion. She preferred to be on top of him like this, because she could control him better. She also didn't like it when he finished in her mouth, so this way was better for her, and as long as she made it good for him, he'd be happy.

"Oooh, baby," she said, sitting back on him, taking him deeper inside of her, flexing her muscles so that she was almost clutching at him with her insides. She knew that when she did this it drove men wild. Ellen had taught her to do it. She knew that when Jackson—and a lot of men—

were ready to go, this was a move that took them over the edge. True to form, Lex Jackson opened his mouth and bellowed as he suddenly exploded and spurted inside of her . . .

Angel walked Jackson downstairs, his hand holding on to her ass tightly. He had already paid Mabel before they went upstairs, but Angel was holding an extra couple of dollars in her fist as she walked him down.

At the door she kissed him and said, "Come back soon, lover. I'll miss you."

"I'll be back, girl," he said. "You can count on it."

He kissed her soundly, slapped her on the rump and then went out the door. When Angel turned, Ellen was standing there. She was brunette, about five years older than Angel's twenty-five, and had a full, lush body that Angel envied. Angel wished she had breasts as large and round as Ellen's.

"Did it work?" Ellen asked.

Angel smiled and said, "It always does." Surreptitiously she showed the older whore her clenched first. She didn't have to tell Ellen what was inside.

"Come with me," Ellen said. "I've got a live one who wants to do two girls at one time. He's a regular, and if we play him right we can both make some extra cash . . ."

Outside Lex Jackson was feeling invincible. He always felt that way after he was with one of his whores. He knew the girls had to fake their passion with the other men, but not with him. That's why he always left Mabel's with his chest puffed out.

It was beginning to get dark as he started to walk back toward the center of Goliad. Mabel's was at the north end of town, and the building stood by itself. That's why it was easy for someone to come out from behind the building and poke a gun into the center of his back.

"What the—"

"Shhh," the person said, digging the gun barrel deeper into his back. A hand snaked out and disarmed him.

"What the hell are you doin'?" he demanded, raising his hands. "Do you know who I am? Who I work for?"

A hand grabbed his arm and pulled him around to face the building again. Then he was pushed toward the building.

"Where we goin'?" he demanded, as he was led behind the cathouse. "Whataya want? My money? You can have it."

He kept talking until they got around back. He looked up at the lit windows, but he knew that everybody in those rooms was too busy to be looking outside.

"Listen," he stated, "let's work somethin'—" He was cut off by a gun barrel striking him on top of the head. He went down to his knees and was hit again before he could raise his hands to protect himself. The second blow drove him to the ground, where he was hit again and again and again . . .

Abigail Drew knew that Mabel didn't like her girls smoking. It wasn't ladylike, she said. Abigail thought that Mabel was a big hypocrite, because all the girls in the house knew that the madam smoked cigars every chance she got.

So whenever Abby needed a cigarette, she'd sneak out of the house for a quick one. She had just sent a lonely cowboy home with a smile on his face—a smile she hoped he would not let his wife see—so she figured she deserved a cigarette break.

She stepped out the back door and found that it had gotten dark early, probably because there was not much of a moon in the sky. She moved away from the house and struck a match to her cigarette. She took a few more steps—not wanting Mabel to see the glowing tip if she happened to look out the window—and proceeded to stumble over something. She fell to her knees, but managed to save her cigarette. She turned to see what she had fallen over, and decided to strike another match to find out. She put the cigarette in her mouth, found another lucifer and struck it on her nail. When she saw the blood and the caved-in skull, she started screaming, and her cigarette fell from her mouth, forgotten.

NINETEEN

The area behind the whorehouse was lit by torches, some being held by deputies, others having been stuck in the ground.

"It's Jackson, all right," Collins said, crouching over the body.

"Goddamnit!" Sheriff Strode said.

"Cal Davis ain't gonna like this," Terry Madison said.

"Shut up, Terry," Strode said.

"But—"

"Go inside and see if anyone else besides Abby saw anything," Strode said.

"Yes, sir."

"And don't let any of those women come out here until we get rid of this body."

"Yes, sir."

Terry turned and hurried toward the house.

"And be professional, damn it!" Strode called after him. "Leave those girls alone."

Terry turned, was about to say something, then simply waved and continued to the house.

After Abby had screamed and screamed until most of the occupants of the house came out to see what was going on, Mabel had sent someone for the sheriff, and had been smart enough to get everyone back into the house.

Strode had sent her messenger to look for his deputies, and was first on the scene. Collins and Terry Madison had arrived shortly thereafter, and Strode had sent them after torches. Judging from the clothes the dead man was wearing, he'd thought it was Lex Jackson, but it wasn't until they'd illuminated the area with torches that they were able to confirm it.

"He's right, you know," Collins said, standing up and wiping his hands on his thighs. "Davis ain't gonna like it, and neither is his boss, the old man."

"Mr. Travis," Strode said.

"If you say so."

Strode walked over and examined the body.

"Somebody was mad at him," he said. "His skull is crushed."

"Probably just a quiet way to kill him, rather than firing a gun," Collins said. "In the absence of a knife, just use your gun to club a man to death."

Strode stood up.

"You send Mabel's boy for the undertaker?" he asked.

"I did."

"Do you know where Clint Adams has been for the past few hours?" the sheriff asked.

"No, I don't," Collins said, frowning, "but you don't think he did this, do you?"

"Why not?" Strode asked. "He's a stranger in town."

"And because he's a stranger, he doesn't even know Jackson," Collins pointed out.

"And you told me that Jackson was watching Adams earlier today, right?" Strode asked. "Maybe our famous Gunsmith doesn't like being watched."

"So he kills a man?" Collins asked.

"I don't pretend to know what makes a man like Clint Adams kill, Collins," Strode said. "I'm gonna have the undertaker move this body and then I want to see Adams in my office. You go and get him."

"What if he doesn't want to come?"

"Make him," Strode said. "You're the one wearin' a badge, not him, remember?"

"Sure, Sheriff."

"And don't ask him any questions," Strode said. "Leave that to me. Just bring him in."

"Yes, sir."

As Collins walked away, Strode stared down at the dead man again. Both deputies were right. Cal Davis wasn't going to like this at all.

Clint was alone in his room, reading a Mark Twain book, when there was a knock on his door. He got up off the bed, removed his gun from the gunbelt hanging on the bedpost and carried it to the door with him.

"Who is it?"

"Steve Collins."

He put the gun behind his back and opened the door.

"Is this official, or unofficial?" Clint asked.

"Official," Collins said, "so you won't be needin' that gun you've got behind your back."

Clint brought the gun into sight and held it down by his leg. "What's going on?"

"The sheriff wants to see you."

"About what?"

"There's been a murder."

"And he wants to see me about it?" Clint asked. "I don't even know anybody in town."

"Remember the man who was watching you earlier today?" Collins asked.

"I remember," Clint said. "You said his name was Jackson."

"Lex Jackson," Collins said, "and that *was* his name. He'd dead."

"How was he killed?"

"Looks like somebody clubbed him to death with a gun barrel."

"Where?"

"Outside the local cathouse. He'd just finished up with one of the girls. Looks like somebody was waitin' outside for him."

"And the sheriff thinks it was me?"

"The sheriff knows you're a stranger in town," Collins said. "That's about all he knows."

"Okay," Clint said. "Come on in while I pull my boots on."

Collins stepped into the room as Clint holstered his gun, sat on the bed and reached for his boots.

"Just between you and me," the deputy said, "I wasn't supposed to tell you nothin', so don't let on that I warned you."

"No problem," Clint said. "I'm obliged."

Once he had his boots on, he grabbed his gunbelt from the bedpost and started strapping it on.

"Maybe I should carry that," Collins said.

"Maybe not," Clint said. "I'm not about to walk around town unarmed, Steve."

Collins shrugged. "It was just an idea."

Clint put his hat on and said, "Lead the way."

"Why don't you walk in front of me?" Collins asked. "It'll look better for me."

"Sure, why not?" Clint asked.

TWENTY

When they reached the sheriff's office, Sheriff Strode was not there yet.

"Probably still seein' to gettin' Jackson over to the undertaker's," Collins said.

"The sheriff must be worried about Jackson's boss and what he's going to be thinking."

"You got that right," Collins said. "Cal Davis ain't gonna be very happy."

"And what about Travis?"

"Jackson worked for Davis," Collins said. "I doubt the old man even knows who he is."

"What's Davis like?"

"Mean," Collins said, "and smart."

"What's his background before he came here?"

"Can't say," Collins said. "I think he's an experienced ramrod, though."

"And how did he get along with his own men?"

"They respect him, I think," Collins said, "or fear him."

"What about Jackson?"

"Jackson was Davis's right-hand man," the deputy said.

"I think he came here with him, so they've worked together before, or at least ridden together. You want some coffee while we wait?"

"Sure."

Collins had just handed Clint a cup when the door opened and the sheriff walked in.

"Why does he have coffee?" he demanded.

"I didn't know how long we'd have to wait—"

"You always give coffee to a suspect in a murder?" Strode demanded.

"I don't know," Collins said, "I haven't dealt that much with murder suspects, Sheriff."

"You want the coffee back?" Clint asked.

"Forget it!" He went to the stove, got himself a cup and walked over to seat himself behind his desk. He kept his gunbelt on rather than hang it on the peg behind him.

"What's this about, Sheriff?"

"He didn't tell you?" Strode demanded, jerking his head toward Collins.

"He hasn't said a word, except to say that you wanted to see me about something," Clint said. "I assume, from what you just said, it's about a murder."

"You know a man named Lex Jackson?"

"No," Clint said, "I don't know him. Wait." He looked at Collins. "Isn't he the man you pointed out to me earlier today? Told me he was watching me?"

"Yeah, that's him," Collins said, knowing their act wasn't fooling the sheriff.

"Look, Adams," Strode said, "this is nothing personal. You're a stranger in town and . . ."

"And what?"

"And you have a certain reputation."

"How was this man killed?"

"He was clubbed to death, maybe with a gun barrel."

"Okay, first of all I've got too much regard for my gun to use it as a club," Clint said, "and second, if I'm going to kill someone it'll be in the street, facing him."

"I didn't say he was clubbed from behind."

"If you're going to club someone to death, are you going to do it so they see it coming?"

"I don't know," Collins said, "I haven't given much thought to clubbing somebody to death."

"You want to check my gun?"

"Sure," the sheriff said. "Hand it over."

Clint took his gun from his holster and handed it over, butt first. The sheriff gave it a cursory examination and then held on to it.

"No blood," he said, "and the barrel doesn't look bent."

"I'll need that back."

"In good time."

"No," Clint said, "now."

"Are you trying to tell me my job?" Strode asked.

"I'm telling you that I'm not about to walk out of here unarmed, Sheriff. That's a sure way to Boot Hill, and I'm not in a hurry to get there." He stuck his hand out.

Strode hesitated, seemed about to say something, and then handed the gun back.

"Thank you." Clint holstered it. "Any suspect besides me?"

"Try anybody who ever did business with old man Travis," Collins said.

"Mr. Travis," Strode said.

"Sorry," Collins said, "*Mr.* Travis."

"Collins, why don't you go and help Terry question the people in Mabel's house. That way we can finish faster and they can go home."

"To their wives," Collins said. "I'll bet that idea thrills them."

He left the office without another word to either the sheriff or Clint, but did give Clint a look that the sheriff missed.

"Mind if I get some more coffee?" Clint asked.

"Sure," Strode said. "Bring the pot over. I can use some more, too. In fact, I could use a drink."

Clint brought the pot over and filled the sheriff's cup.

"Am I really a suspect?" he asked.

Strode took of his hat and ran his hand through his hair.

"I just had to question you," he said.

"Well, if I'm not a suspect and there's a bottle of whiskey in your drawer . . ." Clint raised his cup.

"Why not?"

Strode brought out a bottle of whiskey, tipped a bit into his cup and then into Clint's.

"How much experience do you have with murders?" Clint asked, seating himself.

"Not much," Strode said, "but it's my job. I guess I'll have to go out to the ranch and talk to Cal Davis."

"The foreman?"

"Right."

"What about the boss?"

"Mr. Travis?"

"If that's what he calls himself."

"I don't think he'd know anything about this."

"So you're not going to question him?"

"Adams . . ." Strode took a moment to finish his coffee. "Why don't you move along. I'm done with you."

"Seems to me you have a responsibility to question everybody who knew the dead man—"

"Adams, I didn't ask for your help, and I'm finished questioning you."

"Fine," Clint said. He put his cup down on the sheriff's desk. "Good luck finding your killer."

As Clint went out the door, he thought he heard the sheriff mutter, "I'm gonna need it."

TWENTY-ONE

Clint was in Anderson's saloon later when Steve Collins came walking in with the other deputy, Terry Madison.

"Clint, this is Terry," Collins said, as both deputies joined him at the bar and flanked him. "He wanted to be introduced to you."

"Are you really The Gunsmith?" the young deputy asked.

"That's what they tell me," Clint said. "You boys want a beer, or are you on duty?"

"We're on duty," Collins said, "and we'll take a beer."

The younger deputy continued to stare at Clint as the bartender set beers in front of them.

"How's the investigation going?" Clint asked.

"Beats me," Collins said. "That's the sheriff's problem. All we did was question the girls at Mabel's, and their customers."

"Anybody see anything?"

"Nobody saw anything or heard anything," Madison replied. "At least that's what they say."

"Who found the body?"

"Abby," Madison said. "She's one of the girls. She went outside for a cigarette and tripped over the dead man."

"That must have scared her."

"She screamed and everybody came runnin'."

Clint turned his head and looked at Collins. "I don't think the sheriff is going to question Mr. Travis."

"That's his business."

"He won't be doing his job if he leaves him out," Clint said.

"It doesn't matter," Collins said. "Cal Davis is the one who runs things out there."

"Besides," Madison said, "Mr. Travis is too old to have killed Jackson."

"He could have had it done," Clint said.

"Why?" the young deputy asked. "Why would he have his own man killed?"

"I don't know," Clint said. "That's why you would question him."

"Like I said," Collins replied, "that's up to the sheriff. As he's always reminding us, he's the boss."

Collins finished his beer and set the empty mug down on the bar. "Let's go, Terry."

"I ain't fin—"

"Learn to drink faster, boy. Let's go."

"See you boys tomorrow," Clint said.

"You stayin' in town longer?"

"A few days," Clint said. "My curiosity is up."

"I was you, I'd move on," Collins said. "But that's just me."

"It was a pleasure to meet you, sir," Madison said.

"You, too, Deputy."

Clint watched the two men leave the saloon, then turned and ordered himself another beer.

• • •

"Whataya think?" Terry Madison asked Collins when they were on the street.

"About what?"

"You think he did it?"

"Why would he?"

"Maybe he was hired to," Madison suggested.

"If he was gonna be hired to kill anybody, it would be the old man, don't you think?"

"You always say that."

"Say what?"

" 'The old man,' " Madison said. "You never call him Mr. Travis."

"Do you think he's really William Travis, from the Alamo?" Collins asked.

"I dunno," Madison said, with a shrug. "He says he is."

"People say lots of things."

"You don't believe him?"

"No, I don't," Collins said, "but I don't care. He can call himself George Washington for all I care."

They walked a little farther before Madison asked, "You think the sheriff should question Mr. Travis?"

"I think if the sheriff's gonna run an investigation, he should talk to everyone," Collins said. "But he works for the old man, don't he?"

"We all do, I guess."

"Then I guess he ain't gonna get questioned, is he?"

"But Jackson worked for him," Madison said. "Won't he want the killer found?"

"You'd think."

"Then wouldn't he cooperate?"

"I guess that'll be up to Cal Davis."

"If the sheriff goes out there to talk to either one of them, I wanna go with him, don't you?"

"What for?"

"Maybe to get a look at Mr. Travis."

"One old man looks about the same as another, Terry," Collins said. "Besides, one of us will have to stay in town. You really want to go with the sheriff, I'll volunteer to stay."

"Gee, thanks, Steve."

"Sure," Collins said. "I'm gonna turn in."

"We're supposed to take another turn around town."

Collins walked away with a wave and said, "I'll keep my eyes open all the way to my room."

TWENTY-TWO

Clint finished his second beer and decided to turn in for the night. He had a feeling tomorrow was going to be an eventful day.

He left the saloon and headed for his hotel. He was in the center of the street, crossing over, when two shots rang out and two bullets struck the dirt in the street on either side of him. He went into an immediate roll, and came to stop next to a horse trough, with his gun in his hand. He didn't know what direction the shots had come from, so he wasn't sure if getting behind the trough would do any good. When there were no more shots, he stood up, still warily holding his gun in front of him. About half a dozen men came running out of the hotel, but they didn't leave the boardwalk. They were there to watch, not to help.

Somebody came running from another direction. Clint turned and pointed his gun at Deputy Steve Collins.

"Whoa!" Collins said, holding up his hands.

Clint lowered his gun.

"What happened?" Collins asked.

"Two shots."

93

"From where?"

"I couldn't tell."

"Okay, you take that side of the street, I'll take this side," Collins said. They were about to split up when the sheriff came running up, followed by Terry Madison.

"What the hell—"

"Later," Collins said. "Sheriff, we need the rooftops checked on both sides for a shooter."

"Okay," Strode said, "but then we talk." He turned to Madison. "That side. I've got this one. We'll meet back here. Go!"

Clint checked his side of the street, trying front doors to see if any of them were open, checking alleyways alongside and behind buildings. He came up empty, and returned to the street where he'd left the three lawmen. Collins was already there.

"Still waiting on Terry and the sheriff," he said. "I didn't find anything."

"Me, neither."

"How close did the shots come?"

"One on each side."

Collins looked down at the ground.

"That was bad shooting," he said, "or, considering the dark, real good."

"That's what I was thinking."

Collins looked at the men standing in front of the saloon. They were still watching, waiting for someone to catch a bullet.

"Unless one of you has something useful to say, get on back inside!" the deputy shouted.

All the men turned and went inside, most of them feeling disappointed. The only light on the street was coming from the doorway and windows of the saloon, and both the sheriff and Terry Madison came walking into it from opposite directions.

"Find anything?" Collins asked.

"Nothin'," Strode said.

"Me, neither," Madison said.

"Okay, then," Strode said, looking at Clint, "let's go to my office."

"Again?"

The sheriff looked at Madison and Collins.

"You fellas turn in," Strode said. "Be at work bright and early."

"Okay, Sheriff," Madison said, and walked away.

"If you don't mind," Collins said, "either of you, I'd like to come along."

"I don't mind," Clint said immediately.

Strode thought it over, then said, "Yeah, okay. Come on."

When they were in the office, each with a cup of coffee, Strode said, "Tell me what happened."

"I don't know," Clint said. "I walked out of the saloon, headed for the hotel, and there were two shots."

"Just two?"

"That's it?"

"How close?"

Clint told the sheriff the same thing he had told Collins: one on each side.

"The shooter missed on purpose," he finished.

"What makes you say that?"

"He came too close in the dark for it to be an accident."

"So you think somebody was trying to scare you away?"

"Seems likely."

"From what?"

Clint shrugged. "Out of town, I guess."

"But why?"

"I don't know why," Clint said. "As far as anyone knows, I'm just passing through."

"So you said."

Strode looked at Collins, who shrugged.

"You should worry about the murder you're working on," Clint said.

"This may be connected."

"I don't know how," Clint said.

"That's what I intend to find out," Strode said. "If I find out you're involved—"

"I'm not."

"I told you to stay out of trouble."

"And I tried," Clint said. "All I did was walk across the street."

"And that's exactly my point."

"Look—"

"Okay, okay," Strode said, "it's not your fault somebody took a shot at you. If you were going to your hotel to turn in for the night, why don't you do that now? Steve, walk him there. Get him tucked in safe and sound."

"Yes, sir."

"I'll see you tomorrow," Strode said.

Clint wasn't sure if he was talking to him or to Collins, but he nodded and followed the deputy out the door.

They walked to the hotel without incident, and stopped right in front.

"What are you thinkin'?" Collins asked.

"I haven't got a clue," Clint said, honestly. "Maybe somebody in the saloon recognized me and decided to try to make a big name for themselves."

"Well, you better be careful tonight," Collins said. "They might try again."

"I don't think so," Clint said. "Like I said before, I think it was a . . . warning."

"To do what?"

"I don't know," he said. "Leave?"

"Well, if I was you, then," Collins said, "I'd leave."

"Can't," Clint said. "Not now. Not even if I'd been planning to. Somebody took a shot at me, and I'm going to find out who it was, and why."

"The sheriff told you to stay out of trouble," Collins said. "That plan sounds like stirring up trouble."

"Either way . . . ," Clint said. "I'll find out what I want to find out."

Collins nodded, turned and walked away.

Up in his room Clint looked out the window and wished he could get a message to Eddie Guerrero, but that was going to have to wait until morning.

First a man working for Travis is killed, and then somebody takes two shots at him. Coincidence was something he hated, so these two things had to be connected.

But how?

TWENTY-THREE

The next morning, Clint walked over to Pedro's little café for breakfast. The Mexican was extremely happy to see him and was very expansive about it.

"Señor Adams, so happy to have you back!" He waved his hands about.

"I'm happy to be here, Pedro," Clint said, sitting at a table. "I'm going to put myself in your hands again, my friend."

"Excellent," Pedro said. "Huevos rancheros, I think."

"And a lot of coffee."

"Sí señor," the Mexican cook said. "Coming right up."

Clint wondered how long it had been since people had stopped coming to eat at Pedro's, and how the man could possibly stay in business if it went on any longer.

He could smell when the eggs started cooking, and then Pedro came out with a pot of coffee and a cup.

"Pedro," Clint said. "Remember what we talked about yesterday, concerning your cousin."

"Sí señor."

"I need to speak with him," Clint said. "Can you get a message to him?"

"But of course," the man said. "When do you want this to be?"

"As soon as possible," Clint said.

"I can send someone for him," Pedro said, "and have him here before you finish your breakfast."

"Well," Clint said, "I didn't expect it to be that fast, but that'd be great."

"I will bring your food, and then I will take care of it," Pedro promised.

"Okay, good."

"But . . ."

"But what?"

Pedro looked around, then turned a worried look Clint's way.

"What has he done now?"

"Eddie? He hasn't done anything," Clint said. "I just need his help with something."

"Very well, then," Pedro said. "As long as he hasn't . . . gotten into trouble."

"Not that I know of," Clint said.

"I will bring your food."

"Thanks, Pedro."

Clint concentrated on his coffee while he waited for his food.

Sheriff Strode had woken that morning, dreading the day ahead. First thing he had to do was ride out to the Travis place and talk to Cal Davis. Everything else depended on how Davis reacted. Strode wasn't even sure he'd get to talk to Travis himself.

Now, as he rode up to the house, he was annoyed with himself because he was nervous. This was the only law enforcement job he'd been able to get in the last few years, and he wanted to hold on to it. With Lex Jackson getting shot in town, he knew there was a danger he'd lose it.

As he approached the house, Cal Davis came out the front door, spotted him and came down the stairs to meet him.

"Andy," Davis said. "What brings you out this way?"

It did not escape his notice that that Cal Davis never called him Sheriff.

"I've got some news, Cal," Strode said, dismounting. "It's about Jackson."

"Did he get himself into trouble? Where? At Mabel's?"

"He's dead, Cal."

"What?" Davis looked surprised. "What the hell happened?"

"It was after he finished at Mabel's, last night," Strode said. "Somebody clubbed him from behind and beat him to death out behind the building."

"Somebody? You don't know who?"

"I don't know yet."

"You got a suspect?" Davis demanded. "Did he get into a fight at Mabel's?"

"According to everyone on the place, he did his business and left with no trouble," Strode said.

"Then what? Somebody else in town?"

"This happened late last night," Strode said. "We haven't had time to question people in town. We'll do that today."

Then Davis asked the question Strode had been hoping he would not.

"Are there any strangers in town?"

"Well . . . there's one. I already spoke to him. He and Lex never met, but . . ."

"But what?"

"Lex was watching him."

"Why was Lex watching him? Who is this stranger?"

"His name is . . . it's Clint Adams."

"Adams? What's a man like The Gunsmith doing in Goliad?"

"Just passing through, according to him."

"And Lex was following him?"

"Apparently, but they never spoke."

Davis hesitated, then said, "You know, Mr. Travis isn't going to like it that one of his men was killed in your town."

"If I could talk to him—"

"Forget it," Davis said. "I'll break the news to him. Where's Jackson now?"

"At the undertaker's."

"All right," Davis said. "You get back to town and do your job. Find out who killed him. I'll be along later to see to the body. I've got to check with Mr. Travis and see what he wants to do about this."

"Okay."

"Where's Adams?"

"Still in town."

"Does he plan to stay?"

"He says he's not going anywhere. In fact . . . last night somebody took a couple of shots at him."

"Wait a minute," Davis said. "He's just passin' through and somebody shot at him?"

"It's an occupational hazard with him, Cal."

Davis hesitated a moment once again. "All right, I'll be in town in a while with a few of my boys. I'll have a talk with Clint Adams myself."

"That might not be such a good idea, Cal—"

"I guess I'll decide what's a good idea and what's not, Andy," Davis said, "or Mr. Travis will."

Now it was Strode who hesitated.

"Something else?" Davis asked.

"No," the lawman said, "nothing else."

"Then I'll see you in town."

"Yeah," Strode said, "yeah, I'll see you in town."

TWENTY-FOUR

True to his word, Pedro got Eddie Guerrero to show up at his restaurant before Clint could finish with his breakfast. Of course, it helped that the huevos rancheros were so good he was taking his time eating it.

"Ah," Eddie said, when he came in the door, "my cousin's famous huevos rancheros."

"Have a seat, Eddie," Clint said.

As if on cue, Pedro appeared, carrying another breakfast plate.

"I heard you come in," he told Eddie, and set the plate down in front of him.

"Ah, *gracias,* Pedro."

Pedro had also brought out an empty coffee cup. He set it down, filled it and returned to the kitchen.

"He is a great man, my cousin," Eddie said. "It is a shame he is going to waste here in Goliad."

"Eddie," Clint said, sitting back, "let me see your gun."

"Eh?"

"Your gun," Clint repeated. He put his hand out. "I'd like to examine it."

Eddie stared at Clint for a few moments, then shrugged, removed his gun from his holster and handed it to him butt first. Clint examined the gun for a moment. It was a not-very-well-cared-for Colt, but the barrel was straight and true. The weapon did not look as if it had been used as a club recently.

He handed it back.

"What was that about?" Eddie asked. He had ranchero sauce on his chin.

"Nothing," Clint said. "Forget it. Did you hear about the man who was killed last night?"

"Yes," Eddie said. "Lex Jackson. He was no loss to anyone."

"And that someone took two shots at me?"

Eddie stopped eating.

"I didn't hear that," he said. "Were you hit?"

"No," Clint said. "I think they were just trying to scare me. But I still don't like getting shot at."

"Is that why you sent for me?"

"I want to find out who it was," Clint said. "Who in town would want to scare me away?"

"You want me to guess?"

"Yes."

Eddie thought for a moment, then said, "I can't." He started to eat again.

"Why not?"   •

"Because I can't think of anyone who would care if you leave town or not."

Clint considered Eddie's answer for a moment, then said, "What if I told you I was here to determine if the man who calls himself William Travis is the real thing?"

Eddie stopped chewing again. "Is that really why you are here?"

"If it was, could you make a guess then?"

"If that was why you were really here," Eddie said, "half the town would want to scare you away."

"That's not much better," Clint said.

"But probably someone working for Mr. Travis himself would want it more."

"Like Cal Davis?"

Eddie sat back in his chair.

"If Cal Davis thought you were in his way," he said, finally, "I don't think he would try to scare you out of town by shooting at you."

"No?"

"No," the Mexican said. "He would take a more . . . how do you say . . . direct approach?"

"You mean . . ."

"Cal Davis would just kill you."

TWENTY-FIVE

Cal Davis rode into Goliad with four men riding behind him. All four were men hired by him, who took orders from him and wouldn't have known anyone named William Travis if they saw him. They were also all friends of Lex Jackson.

Davis led them to the sheriff's office, where he dismounted.

"Just wait here," he told them, handing the reins of his horse to Bob Gregg.

"Yessir."

Davis entered the sheriff's office, startling both Sheriff Strode and Deputy Terry Madison. On the other hand, Steve Collins just gave the man a bored look over the rim of his coffee cup. He was in his favorite position, one hip perched on a desk.

"Where's Adams?" Davis asked.

"I don't know," Strode said. "If he's not at his hotel, he's probably out having breakfast."

"Where?"

"Pedro's would be a good guess," Strode said. "At least, he ate there yesterday."

Davis looked around at all three men, and then back at Strode. "I thought we said nobody was to eat there."

"Nobody from town," Steve Collins replied. "Adams is not from town."

Davis glared at Collins, who looked unscathed by it.

"I'll find him. Just keep your boys out of my way, Strode."

"You gonna face him alone, Cal?" Collins asked.

"I got four of my best boys with me."

"That's just askin' for trouble, Cal," Strode said. "Maybe you should talk to him alone first."

"Don't try to tell me what to do, Andy," Cal Davis said. "Just keep out of my way."

With that, he turned on his heel and stalked out of the office. Collins put his coffee cup down and stood up.

"Where you goin'?" Strode asked.

"I'm just gonna watch from a safe distance."

"You stay here, Collins."

"It's five-to-one, Sheriff," Collins said. "Those odds could get even a gunsmith killed."

Strode started to say something, stopped, then said, "Okay, then, go and watch."

"I'll go, too," Madison offered.

"You stay here, Terry," Strode said.

"But, Sheriff—"

"Just do like I tell you!"

"Yessir," Madison said, morosely.

"I'll report back," Collins said, and left the office.

TWENTY-SIX

Eddie Guerrero had just gone into the kitchen to talk to Pedro when the doorway seemed to fill up with men. Clint looked up from his last cup of coffee and saw the men crowding the door. Only one of them walked into the place, though. The rest took up position outside.

The man who entered walked to the table and fronted Clint.

"Can I help you?" Clint asked.

"You Adams?"

"That's me."

"My name's Cal Davis," the man said. "That mean anything to you?"

"Beyond the fact that I've heard your name once or twice since I came to town," Clint said, "no, it doesn't."

"Well, it should mean somethin'," Davis said. "I ramrod the Travis place."

"Travis," Clint said. "Oh yeah, I've heard his name, too. If you've got something you want to say to me, Mr. Davis, why don't you sit down and say it?"

"I can say what I have to say standin' up."

Clint looked past the man at his four colleagues waiting outside. They all wore guns and looked like they knew how to use them. If Davis called them inside, Clint was going to be in trouble facing five men in a cramped space.

"Okay, say it."

"If I find out you had anything to do with killin' my man, you're gonna pay for it."

"I didn't even know your man, Davis," Clint said. "I don't have any reason to kill men I don't know unless they come at me, which means I kill them face-to-face. I've never killed a man from behind in my life."

"Well, if I come at you," Davis said, "you'll see it."

Clint made a point now of leaning over to look at the men milling about outside the door.

"And would you be coming alone?"

"I want to know what you're doin' in town."

Clint leaned back in his chair.

"Why is everybody so interested in what I'm doing?" he asked.

"I don't know about anybody else," Davis said. "I want to know if it has anything to do with my boss."

"Your boss?" Clint asked. "I heard you were the boss."

"I told you," Davis said, "I ramrod for Mr. Travis."

"The Ghost of Goliad."

"Don't call him that," Davis warned. "He doesn't like it. He's no ghost."

"Tell me something, Davis," Clint said. "I hear he's the same Travis who was at the Alamo. Is that true?"

"He is who he says he is," Davis said.

"Well, that would make him pretty old, wouldn't it?"

"He's along in years," the foreman said, "but he still has his wits about him."

"So he sent you into town to find out who killed one of his men?" Clint asked.

"I came on my own," Davis said. "It's my job to see to my men."

"Guess you should have spent a little more time seeing to this one. Maybe he wouldn't be dead now."

Davis pointed a finger at Clint. "Like I said," Davis replied, "if I find out you killed him—"

"Start looking and pointing somewhere else, Davis," Clint said. "I had nothing to do with it. And in the future, I'll answer questions that come from the sheriff, not from you."

"You'll answer any question I put to—"

"I think it's time for you to leave," Clint said. "I'd like to finish my last cup of coffee in peace."

Davis stared at Clint and grew red in the face. For a moment Clint thought the man was going to explode, but the foreman regained his composure.

"You'd just better hope it isn't the last cup of coffee you ever have in your life," the man said, finally.

"Okay," Clint said, holding the cup up in front of him, "I've been duly warned and sufficiently frightened."

Davis stared at Clint for a few moments more, then turned and stalked out of the restaurant.

Across the street, Deputy Steve Miller watched and waited. At the first sound of a shot he was ready to cross the street, but if he did that he might find himself running into a hail of lead. He was trying to come up with an alternate plan when he saw Cal Davis come back out of the restaurant without a shot having been fired. He was surprised that Clint Adams and Cal Davis could have had a conversation without someone firing at least one shot. Threats had probably flown both ways, though. Cal Davis was good at threats.

Collins wondered if Davis had actually found himself intimidated by The Gunsmith.

• • •

Cal Davis left the restaurant looking calm, but feeling rage inside. The rage was not at Adams, but at himself for being intimidated by the man. How else could he explain letting the man speak to him the way he had? Any other man would have been dead by now.

"What happened, Boss?" Bob Gregg asked. "You didn't need us in there with you?"

"Shut up!" Davis said. "Get mounted. We're goin' over to Mabel's to ask some questions."

"Mabel's," one of the other men said, his eyes lighting up.

"You'll be staying outside with the horses, Styles," Davis told him.

"Aw, Boss—"

"Forget it, Styles," Gregg said. He was the only one who had worked with Davis long enough to know what was going on inside the man right now. "Don't push it."

He looked at all the other men to give them the same message. In the end they all followed behind Davis without a word.

After Davis left, Eddie Guerrero and Pedro reappeared from the kitchen. Pedro was sweating, and Clint didn't think it was from the heat coming from his stove.

"I thought you were going to shoot up my place," he said, wringing his hands.

"You did not make a friend today, señor," Eddie said. "Davis will not forget, or forgive, the way you spoke to him."

"He's lucky I didn't take it out on him that he made my last cup of coffee get cold." Clint looked at Pedro and raised his cup and his eyebrows at the same time.

"I will refill you," Pedro said, hurrying to the kitchen for a fresh pot of coffee.

As Pedro went to the kitchen, Eddie sat across from Clint again and stared at him.

"What?" Clint asked.

"He left the rest of his men outside this time," Eddie told Clint. "Next time you will have to watch all five—and some of them will be behind you."

"You mean he won't come straight at me like he promised?"

"Oh, he will be in front of you," Eddie said, "but his men will be behind you."

Clint left Pedro's that morning puzzled. He'd apparently met everyone there was to meet in this town, except for the man himself. And when he did meet him, then what? If the man claimed to be William Travis, how was he supposed to disprove it?

He stepped down into the street and crossed over warily. He was still smarting from the shots that had been fired at him the night before. He should have reacted in time to locate the shooter. The fact that he didn't made him feel like he was slowing down.

He decided to leave it Eddie Guerrero to find information on the dead man and who might have killed him— Eddie and the sheriff. His job was to confirm Travis's claim about who he was, and he wasn't going to be able to do that in town.

He walked the length of the town to the livery without encountering Davis and his men, or any of the lawmen. Inside, he saddled Eclipse. When he walked him out, he encountered the liveryman, walking a tired horse behind him.

"Not looking to buy another horse, are you?" the man asked. Then when he saw Eclipse, he added, "No, I guess not."

"Can you tell me the way to the Travis ranch?"

The older man stared at him with rheumy eyes and asked, "You a friend of Mr. Travis?"

"No," Clint said, "but I'm looking forward to meeting him."

"Not too many people get to do that, but I guess you're welcome to try," the man said. "Sure, can tell ya how to get there . . ."

TWENTY-SEVEN

When Clint saw the house, he reined Eclipse in. Davis and his men were still in town, but there were other men working on the ranch. Some of them were spread out around the place, others probably off in different parts of the ranch.

It couldn't be this easy to get to Travis, though.

Paul Kerry spotted the lone rider coming toward the house and called to some of the other men.

"Rider comin' in!"

Two other men came to join him, and they stood at the foot of the steps that led to the front door. Kerry had orders from Cal Davis that nobody was to get in to see Mr. Travis. He was wearing a gun on his hip, and the other two men were armed with rifles.

"Don't do anything unless I say so. Got it?" Kerry said.

"Got it," one of the other men said, and the second one nodded.

They stood their ground and waited.

• • •

Clint saw the three men form a line in front of the stairs. Apparently, the foreman had left instructions behind. He kept his horse moving forward and stopped about ten feet from them.

"Hello," he said.

"Who are you?" one of them demanded. He was standing in the center, wearing a gun. The other two flanked him, holding rifles. Only the men in the center looked as if he knew how to handle the weapon.

"I'm here to see Mr. Travis."

"Nobody gets in to see Mr. Travis."

"What's your name?" Clint asked.

"Paul Kerry."

"I'm Clint Adams. I saw your boss in town. He told me I could come out here and see Mr. Travis."

"That's a lie," Kerry said. "Cal would never tell you that."

One of the other men nudged him and said, "He's The Gunsmith."

"Shut up."

The other man said, "I didn't sign on to face no gunfighter."

"I said shut up," Kerry said, turning his head to look at the second man.

Clint sat still. He thought the situation might take care of itself, in a minute or two.

The two nervous men looked at him and he smiled.

"To hell with this," one of them said. "I'm gettin' out."

"Me, too," the other one said.

As they started away, Kerry shouted, "You're both fired!"

"We quit," one of them said.

Kerry looked at Clint.

"Now you're all by yourself," Clint said. "Are you good enough to keep me out of the house?"

"W-what do you want?"

"I just want to talk with your boss," Clint said. "And by that I mean Travis, not Cal Davis."

"You ain't here to kill him?"

"I'm not here to kill anyone, Kerry," Clint said. He dismounted, keeping his eyes on the man. "Like I said, I just want to talk."

"Well," Kerry said, lifting his hand away from his gun, "I guess there's no harm in that, is there?"

"No," Clint said, "I guess not." He walked to the nearest hitching post in front of the house and looped Eclipse's reins around it. "My horse better be here when I come out."

"It'll be here."

"Where do I find Mr. Travis?"

"One of two places," Kerry said. "His bedroom on the second floor, or his office in the back of the first."

"Thanks."

"I'm gonna get fired for this."

"I'll put in a good word with Mr. Travis."

Clint mounted the steps, opened the front door and went inside.

Outside Paul Kerry was trying to figure out a way not to get fired, but also not to get killed. He wondered what the rest of the men on the grounds would do for a bonus.

Clint might have been impressed with the size of the house if he'd let himself, but his visit wasn't about that. He didn't know when Cal Davis and his men would be returning, so he had to find Travis quickly. He prowled the first floor, found a hallway leading to the back and followed it. Halfway along he thought he heard someone snoring.

When Clint found the right doorway, he saw an elderly man sitting behind a desk, his chin down on his chest. This was where the snoring was coming from. He was unsure how to act next. Call out the man's name, or walk to he desk and shake him awake? Either way, he was probably going to startle the man.

He was still wondering what to do when the man suddenly lifted his chin from his chest and opened his eyes. He looked directly at Clint.

"Cal?"

"No," Clint said, "I'm not Cal, Mr. Travis."

The man frowned, then wiped one large, long-fingered hand over his face. The skin on his hand was so translucent Clint could see the blue veins running through it.

"Who are you?"

"My name is Clint Adams."

The old man waved his hand in the air and said, "That name means nothing to me."

Clint found that refreshing. It was actually nice to meet someone who had never heard of him.

"No reason it should."

Clint's eyes were drawn to the puckered scar over the old man's left eye. He didn't remember his history, couldn't recall which eye Travis was supposed to have been shot above. But whichever eye it had been, how could the man have survived such a wound?

"Can I help you with something?" the man asked.

"I . . . I . . ." Clint wasn't sure what to say.

"While you're trying to decide," Travis said, "would you get me a glass of port from that sideboard, over there?"

"Sure."

"Get yourself one, too."

"Why not?"

Clint poured two glasses from a crystal decanter, walked over to the old man and handed him one. He noticed Travis's clothes were plain, nothing fancy about them at all. In fact, they looked like work clothes.

"Thank you. Have a seat."

Clint sat across from him and sipped his port. He was sure it was good stuff, but he was far from a good judge of fine wines or liquors.

"How did you get in here?" Travis said. "I don't usually have visitors."

"I'm sure they can't get past you foreman."

"He tries to protect me."

"From what?"

The man thought a moment, then chuckled and said, "I'm not quite sure."

Travis was a tall man, had probably cut a fine figure at one time, but his flesh now hung on his bones without much muscle tone. His eyes had been fuzzy when he'd first awakened, but now that he was drinking the port they seemed clear, and his pallor seems to acquire more color.

"How did you get past him?"

"Oh, he's not here."

"Where is he?"

"In town."

"He didn't tell me he was going to town."

"I think it was sort of an emergency."

"All the more reason he should have told me. What's happening in town?"

"There was a murder."

"Really?" The man frowned. "That's terrible. Who was killed?"

"One of your men," Clint said. "Lex Jackson."

"Jackson." Travis's frown deepened. "I don't know that name. Are you sure he works for me?"

"He works for Cal Davis," Clint said. "I guess that means he works for you, right?"

"I suppose you're right," Travis said. "I don't know all the men Cal has hired."

"If you don't mind me asking . . . when was the last time you were outside?"

Travis turned in his chair and looked out the window.

"It seems like it's been a long time," he said.

Clint looked around the room. It was sparsely furnished, no mementos of any kind. He didn't know what he was expecting to see. Some mortar left over from the Alamo, maybe?

"Mr. Travis."

The old man turned to face Clint. "Yes?"

"Are you really the William Travis who was at the Alamo?" Clint asked.

The older man stared at him for several moments, then said, "That's a good question. A very good question."

Slowly, he reached up and began to stroke the scar over his eye.

TWENTY-EIGHT

Cal Davis came out of Mabel's, shaking his head. Bob Gregg handed him the reins of his horse.

"Anythin', Boss?" he asked.

"Nobody knows nothin'," Davis said.

"What's next?"

"Let's go over to the livery," Davis said. "Maybe there's a stranger in town Strode and his boys missed."

Strode entered his office, and found Steve Collins standing at the stove with a cup of coffee.

"Want one?" Collins asked.

"Thanks."

Strode went behind his desk and Collins handed him a steaming cup.

"Do you know where Adams is?" Strode asked.

"Haven't a clue."

Strode took off his hat and massaged his temples.

"After Davis and his men left him at Pedro's place, I don't know where he went."

"Do you know where Cal went?"

"He and his boys went over to Mabel's."

"They still there?"

"I don't know," Collins said. "I came here."

"If Adams is still in town and they meet up on the street—"

"Maybe he's not in town."

"Where would he be?"

Collins shrugged. "Out to the Travis place?"

"Why would he go there?"

"Why not?" Collins asked. "Davis is in town, isn't he?"

"Do you think that's why he came here?" Strode asked. "To sell his gun to Travis?"

"I don't know why no one can believe he's just passin' through," the deputy said.

"A man like The Gunsmith doesn't just pass through anywhere."

Strode thought for a moment, then put down his coffee, stood up and headed for the door.

"Where are you goin'?"

"I'm gonna ride out there," Strode said. "If Adams is there, then he's lookin' for trouble."

"Want me to come with you?"

"No, stay here and keep an eye on things. I'll be back as soon as I can."

As Strode went out the door, Collins poured himself another cup of coffee. If Adams was out of town, then there wasn't much chance of trouble in town. Time enough for another cup.

At the livery, Cal Davis questioned the liveryman, who told him there were no other strange horses in the stable, except for that big Arabian.

"The Gunsmith's horse?"

"That's right."

Davis looked around. "Where is it?"

"Not here, right now."

"Adams took his horse out?"

"Yep, earlier today."

"Did he leave town?"

"Didn't have his saddlebags with him, if that's what you mean," the man replied. "Fact is, he asked for directions out to your place."

"He rode out to the ranch?"

"I guess."

"Damn it!"

Davis came running out of the livery and said, "Mount up. We're headin' back!"

.

TWENTY-NINE

"The truth is," the old man said, staring down at his hands, "I don't know."

Clint remained silent.

"Cal thinks I am," he went on. "The whole 'Ghost of Goliad' thing was his idea."

"Why not the Ghost of the Alamo?"

The old man looked at Clint.

"That would have been a little too obvious, don't you think?" he asked.

"Probably."

"Cal found me in a town down in Mexico," the man said. "I was almost dead. He told me I was William Travis." He shrugged. "I had no real recollection of who I was."

"What name were you going by when he found you?"

"Smith," the old man said. "What he offered me was much better than what I had, so we came here and started . . . this."

"And are you happy with this?" Clint asked.

"It's better than what I had," Travis said. "I would have been dead in a week."

127

"At least you were probably outside."

That made the old man laugh.

"Oh, I was outside, all right," he said. "Lying on the ground, most of the time, with people stepping over me, or around me."

"What town in Mexico?"

"It's not even there anymore," Travis said. "Somebody sneezed and wiped it out."

"That happens to a lot of towns."

"I suppose it does."

"So you don't have any memories of the Alamo?"

"None."

"Crockett, Bowie," Clint said. "Any of them?"

The old man shook his head. "No memory."

"And when you think about yourself," Clint asked, "are you Smith, Travis . . . or someone else?"

The old man sat back in his chair.

"That's a real good question," he said. "A real good one."

"You got an answer?"

"I don't know," the man said. "Sometimes one, sometimes the other, sometimes . . ."

"Somebody else, altogether. Right?"

"Right."

"You know what I think you need?"

"What?"

"Some fresh air."

"You might be right about that."

THIRTY

When Sheriff Strode came within sight of the Travis ranch, he could see a bunch of ranch hands gathered in front of the house. He could clearly see that many of them were carrying rifles.

"Jesus," he said. He took out his gun, checked the loads, holstered it and headed for the house.

As they walked toward the front door, Clint said, "So what should I call you?"

"I don't know," Travis said. "Are we gonna see each other after today?"

"I don't honestly know."

"Then I guess we don't need to decide that just yet."

They walked at the older man's pace, which was halting. Clint had offered to support the man, but his offer had been declined.

"If I can't walk, I might as well just give up," the old man had said.

Clint had seen his point.

When they reached the front door, Clint opened it and

129

held it while the old man stepped outside, and then he followed.

"Well," the old man said, "quite a reception."

Clint saw the man he had spoken to earlier, this time flanked by almost a dozen men.

"I don't think they're here to greet you, sir."

Paul Kerry had promised each man a bonus if they stood with him against Clint Adams. He had not, however, told them Clint's name, just that a man was in with Mr. Travis and was there to cause trouble.

When the door opened, Kerry said, "Get ready."

When the old man stepped out, it was the first time many of them had ever seen "William Travis."

"What's going on?" the old man asked.

"That man doesn't belong here, Mr. Travis," Paul Kerry said. "We're here to see that he leaves."

The old man peered down at Kerry, then said, "Come up here where I can see you better."

"Yes, sir."

Kerry came halfway up the stairs.

"You're . . . Kerry, right?"

"Yes, sir."

"Mr. Kerry," the old man said, "this man is my guest. Disperse your men."

"But, sir, Cal said no one was to get in to see you."

"Well, you've already failed to keep that from happening, haven't you?"

"Uh, well, yes, sir."

"Tell your men to get back to work."

"Sir, I—"

They were interrupted by the appearance of another rider. Clint could see the sun glinting off the sheriff's badge.

"The sheriff," he said to the old man.

Kerry turned to face the rider, but remained on the stairs.

Strode didn't like the tableau he came riding upon. Too much potential for disaster. He decided to try to make an impression, so he rode his horse right into the midst of the armed men, forcing them to scatter.

"All right, all you men put up your guns and go on back to work," he ordered.

"Sheriff," Kerry said, from the stairs, "you got no right—"

"I'll arrest any man who doesn't obey me," the lawman shouted, "and I'll start with you, Kerry."

Kerry fell silent.

"Now, the man standing there with your boss is called Clint Adams," he said. "That name ring a bell for anyone?"

The men began to mutter and mill about.

"Anyone want to take a chance against The Gunsmith?"

It became obvious that nobody did. Guns were lowered and the men began drifting away. Some of them were casting dirty looks Kerry's way for not telling them who they had almost faced.

Strode turned his attention to Kerry.

"You, too, Paul. Come down from there and go back to work."

Kerry hesitated.

"Do as the sheriff says, Mr. Kerry," the old man said, "or you're fired."

Kerry turned to look at his boss, then said, "Yes, sir." He walked down the stairs and followed in the wake of the other men.

Strode dismounted and came halfway up the stairs.

"Is this man bothering you, Mr. Travis?"

"This man is my guest, Sheriff," the man said. "We've been talking, and we had some port."

"That's all?"

"That's all. I'm afraid there's really no need for you to be here."

"Maybe not."

They all heard the approaching horses and looked up to see five men riding hell-bent for leather their way.

"And them again . . . ," Strode said.

THIRTY-ONE

Cal Davis led his men right up to the front steps, where Strode, Clint Adams and the man he called William Travis were standing.

"What's going on?" he demanded.

"Not much," Strode said. "Seems Mr. Adams and your boss were just havin' a nice visit, and everybody else got kind of upset for nothin'."

"Mr. Travis?"

"Everything is fine, Cal," Travis said. "But I am quite tired. I think it's time for me to go back inside."

"I'll take you," Cal said, dismounting and handing his reins to Gregg. "Get the horses taken care of, and get the boys back to work."

"Yes, sir."

Davis came up the steps and stopped in front of Clint. "Please don't leave. I'd like to talk to you."

"Sure."

"Mr. Adams," the old man said, "it was a pleasure."

Clint shook hands with the man, and noticed that the handshake was surprisingly firm.

Once Davis took the older man inside, and the rest of the hands had dispersed, there was only Clint and the sheriff left.

"What were you thinkin', comin' out here?" Strode asked.

"Hey," Clint said, "nobody wants to believe I'm just passing through, and everybody is threatening me. I just thought I'd come out here and see the man who's supposed to be in charge."

"So what did you find out?" Strode asked.

Clint stared at the sheriff for a few moments, then asked, "You don't know if he's really Travis from the Alamo, do you?"

"How could I?" Strode asked. "I wouldn't know Travis if I saw him. All I know is he claims to be that Travis."

"Well, I don't know, either," Clint said. He didn't mention that Travis himself didn't seem to know any more than they did.

Strode looked around, then back at Clint.

"You gonna wait for Davis?" he asked.

"Why not? He seems to only want to talk. You don't think he'll set his dogs on me right here on the Travis ranch, do you?"

"I don't know what Cal Davis will or won't do," the lawman said. "But if you want to stay here alone, far be it from me to stop you. I just don't want trouble in my town. They wanna kill you here, that's their business."

Strode turned, walked to his horse and mounted up.

"I'm flattered that you rode all this way to save me, Sheriff," Clint said.

"I rode out here to make sure you didn't kill the old man," Strode said. "I don't much care what happens to you, Adams."

"Well," Clint said, "I guess I'll be seeing you in town, then."

Strode shrugged, turned his horse and started back to Goliad.

Cal Davis got the old man up to his bedroom, where he removed his boots for him and stretched him out on his bed.

"Now, this is important, sir," he said, speaking softly. "What did you tell Adams?"

"I told him nothing, Cal," Travis said, "because I know nothing."

"Good."

By the time Davis reached the door, the old man was asleep and snoring. On the stairs going back down, Davis realized he should have asked the man if he'd told Adams that he knew nothing.

Clint turned as the front door opened and Cal Davis stepped out.

"What did you think you were doin'?"

"That's the second time somebody's asked me that question," Clint said.

"And what's your answer?"

"I just wanted to talk to the old boy."

"And what did you find out?" Davis asked. "Anything useful?"

"He's a pretty confused old man."

"That he is," Davis said. "When I found him, he didn't even remember that he was William Travis."

"Of the Alamo."

"Yes."

"But you knew."

"Yes, I did."

"How?"

"That doesn't matter."

"How would you recognize him?"

Davis walked to the edge of the top step and looked off into the distance. "I think it's time for you to leave, Mr. Adams. I hope you appreciate the fact that you're still alive."

"That's a fact I always appreciate, Davis," Clint said.

"Well, if we run into each other in town again—"

"Don't bother threatening me," Clint said.

"It's not a threat."

"You've got that old man wrapped around your little finger, Davis," Clint said. "Maybe he cares what you have to say, but I don't."

Clint went down the stairs and uncoiled Eclipse's reins from the hitching post. He mounted up and looked back at Davis.

"You want to face me in town, I'll be happy to oblige," Clint said. "Just leave your friends behind and do it like a man."

Without waiting for a response, he turned Eclipse and rode away, not very much the wiser. If the old man himself couldn't be sure whether or not he was William Travis, how could Clint be sure enough to tell Don Carlos yes or no?

THIRTY-TWO

Clint returned to town thinking he'd been pretty lucky. He couldn't remember the last time he'd faced that many guns in one day without a shot being fired.

"Mr. Davis find ya?" the liveryman asked, when he handed over Eclipse.

"Oh yeah," Clint said, "he found me. Thanks."

Clint left the livery and went to Anderson's saloon for a cold beer.

"Expected you back before this," Anderson said, putting a beer in front of him.

"Oh yeah? Why's that?"

"Only place in town you can get a real cold beer," Anderson said, "and whiskey that won't eat out your insides."

"I'll pass on the whiskey," Clint said, picking up the beer, "but I need this."

"Bad day?"

"And it isn't over yet."

"Guess you ain't passin' through as easy as you thought, huh?" the bartender asked.

"I guess not."

Clint downed half the beer and set the mug down easily. It was midday, still too early for the saloon to be full. There were a few men there, but he was pretty sure none of them worked for Cal Davis.

"I'm going to drink the rest of this in the back," he said, and Anderson nodded as he walked to a back table and sat down.

Sheriff Andy Strode was standing outside his office when he saw Clint Adams come walking from the direction of the livery and enter Anderson's saloon.

The door opened behind him and Steve Collins came out. Strode had already filled him in on what had happened out at the ranch.

"Your buddy made it back," Strode said.

"I told you, he ain't my buddy."

"Well, he's in Anderson's," the sheriff said. "Why don't you go over there and find out what else happened out there after I left!"

"Sure," Collins said, "why not? I could use a beer."

He stepped down off the boardwalk and started across the street to the saloon.

Clint allowed Anderson to bring him a fresh beer, and decided to work on this one more slowly. He was wondering if he should just send a message to Don Carlos and Elizabeth Vargas now and tell them what he had found out. Which was . . . nothing. Except for the fact that "William Travis" was a rather confused but well-mannered old man who was apparently being manipulated by Cal Davis.

He looked up as the batwing doors opened and Steve Collins walked in. The deputy went to the bar, got himself a cold beer and then walked over to Clint's table.

"Mind if I join you?"

"Strode send you over to question me?"

"What if he did?"

"You're right," Clint said. "Sit down."

Collins pulled out a chair and seated himself. "I heard about what happened out there."

"A lot of guns," Clint said, "but nothing really happened."

"But you got to talk to Travis."

"That I did."

"And you got him to come outside?"

"He needed some air."

Collins waited a few moments, then said, "So?"

"So what?"

"Is he or isn't he William Travis, of the Alamo?"

"Truthfully?"

"Well, yeah, truthfully."

"I don't know."

"Well . . . did you ask him?"

"He's old," Clint said, "and kind of confused."

"You sayin' he doesn't know if he's Travis?"

"I'm saying he doesn't have much of a memory left," Clint said. "I don't think he's got much of anything left."

"So Cal Davis is runnin' things, like we all thought?"

"Looks that way."

"Well . . . what's the difference?" Collins said, sitting back. "It doesn't change things for anybody in this town."

"I guess not."

"But you're not here for anyone in this town, are you?" Collins asked.

"Who do you think I'm here for?"

"If I had to guess one person," Collins said, "I'd say Don Carlos Vargas."

"Why him?"

"Because he's the only other person I know who claims to be a living survivor of the Alamo—from the winning side. Seems to me he'd have an interest in finding out the truth."

Clint made no comment.

"He probably sent his daughter Elizabeth to talk to you," Collins went on. "She's a real beauty, hard to resist."

"So I hear."

"You're sayin' you don't know them?" Collins asked. "Never met them?"

"I'm not saying anything, Steve."

"Well," Collins said, "like I said, it don't make no never mind to anybody in this town. Whether Travis is runnin' things or Davis is, it's all the same."

He lifted his mug, drained it and set it down.

"I got work to do," he said. "That doesn't change, either."

He started out, then turned back.

"Sounds to me like you lucked out today, Clint," he said. "Even you could not have faced off against that many guns and walked away."

"Thanks for that analysis of my abilities, Steve."

"What are you gonna do for the rest of the day?" Collins asked.

"I'm going to find some dinner in a little while, and then probably go to my room."

"You got a lot of thinkin' to do, huh?"

Clint regarded the deputy for a few seconds, then said, "I've got some, that's for sure."

"Well . . . good luck."

THIRTY-THREE

Clint had dinner at Pedro's and told the man everything that had happened that day. The Mexican cook was fascinated, and wanted to know what the Ghost of Goliad looked like.

"He didn't look like much of a ghost to me," Clint said. "He just looked like a tired old man."

"What did he say?" Pedro asked. "Was he at the Alamo?"

"I don't know, Pedro." Clint still hadn't decided to pass on to anyone exactly what he and the old man had talked about. He'd give that to Don Carlos and Elizabeth, when the time came.

"What about Eddie?" Clint asked. "Have you seen him today?"

"No," Pedro said, "not since this morning."

"I hope I haven't put him in too much danger."

"Eddie can take care of himself, señor," Pedro said, almost proudly. "He is very capable."

"I hope you're right, Pedro."

"Don't worry, señor," the man said. "I know my cousin. He will do well for you."

141

"I'll take your word for it."

After a piece of pie and a cup of coffee, Clint left Pedro's, with the promise to return for breakfast.

"That is very good," Pedro said, gratefully, "since you are all my business now."

Clint left Pedro's and started for Anderson's for another beer. Along the way, though, he passed the other saloon—the Mexican cantina—he'd been in before, and decided to stop there instead.

After all, it had two things Anderson's didn't have.

As it turned out Carmen and the older woman from the cantina, Rosa, were neither mother and daughter nor sisters. They just happened to look a bit alike, which—when it came right down to it—made it easier to take them both to bed.

Clint decided to go into the cantina because he felt he needed a diversion—something to take his mind off of things for a while. He got himself a lukewarm beer and then turned to watch the two women work the room. When they spotted him, they both quickly came over to him and he assumed that, somehow, they had found out who he was.

"You're a bad man," Rosa said to him.

"No, I'm not," he said. "In fact, I'm not wanted—"

"She means," Carmen said, pressing up against him, "you are bad for not introducing yourself to us."

He could feel the heat of her body through her dress, and her breasts pressed solidly up against him. But it was the older woman who interested him even more, as her body was more lush and full then the younger woman's.

"Perhaps the señor would be interested in some company?" Rosa asked.

"Perhaps . . . ," Clint agreed.

The women were interested in going to bed with a legend, so there was no charge, and Clint was interested in spending some time in mindless pursuits, so he didn't care what they're motives were. It worked for everyone.

He went back to his hotel and made sure he had at least a bottle of tequila in his room by the time they arrived. They had to wait until the cantina closed, but assured him that they would turn away any other advances and come to his room shortly thereafter.

True to their word, there was a knock on his door in the wee hours, rousing him from a light doze. Although he was expecting them, he still answered the door holding his gun. This not only delighted them, but aroused them, as well.

"I do not think you will need the gun, Señor Adams," Rosa said. "We are already here."

Carmen closed the door while Clint walked to the bed and holstered the gun. When he turned to face them, he knew it was going to be a memorable night. They were already undressing each other, peeling down dress straps from smooth shoulders, revealing full breasts with large, brown nipples.

When the women had stripped each other completely they began to touch each other, but while they're hands were on each other—stroking the underside of a breast, tweaking a nipple—their hot gazes were on Clint.

"You are a little behind, Señor Clint," Carmen said.

"Yes," he agreed, "yes, I am. Maybe you ladies could lend me a hand . . . or two?"

In moments he had two naked women pulling his clothes off of him. By the time he was naked, he was also fully awake, and fully hard.

Carmen knelt in front of him and began caressing his cock, holding it in both hands, stroking it, cooing to it, while Rosa was behind him, pressing her smooth lips to his buttocks, stroking the backs of his thighs and reaching up between his legs to fondle his testicles.

They gravitated toward the bed and fell onto it together. The women both tugged at him, getting him on his back and then crawling on him. Carmen kissed him, thrusting her tongue into his mouth, running her hands over his chest, while Rosa slid down between his legs and began to kiss his erect penis. Later, he would recall the night in stages . . .

. . . Carmen seated on his chest, her vagina pressed to his eager mouth, while Rosa's mouth was sliding up and down his rigid cock. Carmen was moaning, crying out as his tongue and lips did their work, bringing her to a tasty, gushing completion as he erupted into Rosa's avid mouth . . .

. . . Carmen on her back, her legs spread wide as he fucked her, taking her in long, slow strokes while Rosa pressed herself to his back, urging him on. Her full breasts were flattened as much as they could be against his back, the rigid nipples scraping him. She continued to stroke him, rubbing his back and his butt as he slid in and out of Carmen wetly, and at one point she reached between them to encircle the base of his cock with two fingers, actually helping him fuck her friend . . .

. . . still later it was Rosa, the older woman, on her back, her ankles up around her ears as he fucked her with quick hard strokes that drove the breath from her, filling the air with the sound of their wet flesh slapping together.

Carmen laid beside them, alternately stroking both of them, first Clint's face, then Rosa's breasts, Clint's back, Rosa's belly . . . At one point she was tugging on Rosa's distended nipples as he continued to move in and out of her, then slid her fingers down in her pubic bush and beyond, increasing the sensations already being caused by

Clint's continued attentions. Rosa gave in at that point, bit her lips to try to keep silent, but lost the battle as her orgasm overtook her and she cried out loudly, and then again when Clint followed her over the edge . . .

Oddly, sometime during the night, Carmen disappeared, not only from the bed, but from the room, leaving Clint alone with Rosa, to enjoy the older woman's body fully.

When he awoke and found Carmen gone, he looked at Rosa. She was awake, and watching him.

"What happened to Carmen?"

"I sent her away."

"Why?"

"Because she is a child," Rosa said, sliding up next to him, "and you need a woman."

She kissed him, pressing her lush body to his, sliding her hand down between his legs.

"We needed some time alone," she whispered against his mouth.

"I agree," he said . . .

THIRTY-FOUR

Clint turned Rosa over onto her back and got himself comfortable between her parted thighs. He kissed her mouth, then her neck, shoulder and breasts, where he lingered over her delightfully chewy nipples. He lingered there for some time, enjoying the way her heavy breasts fell to the side as she lay on her back, and the way she gasped and sighed as he kissed and licked her. From there he moved down over her ribs, paused at her deep, shadowy navel, and then moved down even further. He slid so that he was lying between her legs. Her thighs were slightly heavy, but the skin was so smooth and silky beneath his lips that he spent some time kissing them and rubbing his face on them. But finally he pressed his face to her fragrant pubic bush. The hair was very black and there was a lot of it, but not so much that it kept him from finding her moist portal. It was hot, wet and waiting. He slid his hand beneath her to cup her chunky buttocks, lifted her slightly and began to eat her.

She started to speak in Spanish. At first he thought she was actually talking to him, but then he realized she was simply speaking as a result of what he was doing. Whether

147

it was for him or for herself he didn't know, because he couldn't understand her, but soon it didn't matter. He became so engrossed in the taste and smell of her that he couldn't hear her anymore.

Soon her belly began to tremble, and then her legs began to jerk. Finally, she was bucking beneath him as waves of pleasure overtook her. Abruptly, he got to his knees, turned her over and entered her from behind, sliding up between her thighs and into her soaking vagina. She bucked back against him with each thrust, so that he plunged deeply into her with each stroke, and when it finally came time for him to finish, they cried out together in a duet of pleasure . . .

"You were right," he told her later.

"About what?"

She was lying with her head on his shoulder. He had an arm around her so that he could cup one firm breast.

"About sending Carmen away," he said. "She's a beautiful girl, but you are a lovely, experienced woman, and I'm thoroughly enjoying my time with you."

She chuckled and said, "It is not over yet, Señor Clint. Of that I assure you."

He laughed with her and said, "I never thought it was, Rosa. There's still a lot of the night ahead of us."

They put the rest of the night to good use, getting very little sleep, and it wasn't until the sun started to come up, and Rosa slipped from the bed, dressed, kissed Clint and left, that he finally fell asleep for a couple of hours.

When he awoke, there was the most pleasant feeling of fatigue in his loins, and despite the fact that he'd slept very little, he felt refreshed. It had been hours since he'd given any thoughts to the Alamo, Cal Davis or an old man who was called William Travis.

• • •

When Cal Davis woke the next morning, it was with the unshakable feeling that Clint Adams had found out more during his visit the previous day than the old man had let on. And yet, what did the old man even know to tell?

With the death of Lex Jackson, Davis no longer had a confidante, or an accessory. He was going to have to find someone new to fill that job, and that was how he intended to spend the morning. But later, when the old man was awake and alert, they were going to have another long talk.

Clint appeared at Pedro's for breakfast, and the man was waiting for him.

"Señor," Pedro said, as he served breakfast, "you must tell me everything that happened yesterday. My curiosity eats away at me."

"Not much to tell, Pedro," Clint said. He told the Mexican cook about all the men with guns he'd faced while out at the Travis place, but he did not tell him what he and the old man had discussed. For the time being he was keeping the old fellow's apparent amnesia to himself. He still hadn't figured whether or not he wanted to fill Don Carlos in just yet on what he'd found.

When he was finished with breakfast, Pedro took his money and said gravely, "My cousin has asked you to meet with him this morning at the livery stable."

"Eddie?"

"Sí."

"What's on his mind?" Clint asked. "Has he found out something about the murder?"

"I do not know, señor," Pedro said, with a shrug. "I simply pass on the message."

"All right, Pedro," Clint said. "I'll go and see what he wants. Thanks."

"Thank you, señor," Pedro said. "I will be saddened when you leave, for I will have no one else to cook for."

"Maybe that won't be the case, Pedro," Clint said. "Maybe, by then, things will have changed in Goliad."

"From your lips to God's ears, señor."

THIRTY-FIVE

Wary of another trap, Clint walked to the livery stable to meet with Eddie Guerrero. When he arrived, Eddie was leaning against a wall, smoking a cigarette. When he saw Clint enter the stable, he dropped the cigarette to the floor and carefully crushed it with his heel.

"I would not want to start another fire," he said, matter of factly.

"Another fire?"

Eddie waved the subject away.

"That was a long time ago," he said. "It is not something that needs to be brought up now."

"Have you found something out that will help me now, Eddie?" Clint asked.

"I think so, señor," Eddie said.

When he was not immediately forthcoming with the information, Clint said, "And are you going to tell me what it is?"

"Of course, señor," Eddie said. "Why else would I be here?"

"I was wondering that myself," Clint said, shaking his head. "All right, out with it, then."

"Elizabeth Vargas, she is in town."

"So?" Clint asked. "When did she get here? Today?"

"She has been here for several days."

Clint frowned. He doubted that a woman who looked like Elizabeth Vargas could have been in Goliad for days without him seeing her. On top of the fact that she was a big, beautiful woman, she tended to dress in colors that could be seen for miles. The only way she could have gone unnoticed was if she'd wanted to.

"She's been hiding?"

"*Sí.*"

"So that I wouldn't know she was here."

"*Sí.*"

"Why would she do that?"

"Normally, I would not tell you, señor," Eddie said.

"But why now?"

Eddie shrugged and said, "I do not like the way she and her father are using you."

"Using me?"

"To find out if the old man is truly William Travis."

"You know about that?"

"But of course. Why else would they have asked me to help you while you are in town?"

"I thought they might have kept you in the dark about the reasons I was here."

"Señor," Eddie said, shaking his head, "it is you who are being kept in the dark."

"I'm starting to see that, Eddie," Clint said. "Can you tell me where she's been staying?"

"I cannot," Eddie said. "But if you were to follow me and find out for yourself, how would I know that?"

"I understand, Eddie," Clint said. "Thank you."

"*Por nada, señor,*" Eddie said. "Men like Don Carlos think they're money entitles them to anything, and women like the señorita think they're beauty entitles them to the same thing. Me, I am not so wealthy, or so pretty, and I suspect neither are you."

"You've got that right."

"Then we must—how do you say—stick together?"

"Yes, Eddie," Clint said, "stick together."

"I must go and report to the señorita now, señor," Eddie said. "If you would excuse me?"

"Of course, Eddie."

"*Gracias,*" Eddie said. "I will see you later."

Clint waited for Eddie to leave, then followed discreetly behind him. He didn't know whom he could trust, but if Eddie had been trying to set him up for an ambush, he could have done it very easily in the stable.

He followed Eddie down several streets until the man stopped in front of a two-story wood-frame house that looked large enough to be used as a rooming house. Clint took up a position across the street and watched as Eddie went to the door and knocked.

The door was opened by an elderly woman. Eddie spoke to her briefly, and then she closed the door. After a few moments the door opened again and Clint could clearly see Elizabeth Vargas standing in the doorway. She was easy to see, with her great mane of hair and the purple shirt she was wearing.

They spoke for a few moments, Eddie gesturing with his hands, Elizabeth adopting a posture of what seemed to Clint to be superiority, hands on hips, head cocked, as if she were enduring what Eddie had to tell her.

Finally, she spoke to Eddie and did some gesturing of

her own, then backed up and almost slammed the door in his face. Eddie turned, remained on the doorstep for a moment, then gave a shrug that no one would guess had been directed at Clint. He returned down the walk and headed into town, without looking back.

Clint left his position, crossed the street to the big house, went up to the door himself and knocked. Elizabeth must have thought it was Eddie again, for she jerked the door open, an angry look on her face. When she saw it was Clint, she stopped short and stared.

"Oh," she said.

"That's right," Clint said. "Oh. Can I come in?"

THIRTY-SIX

"You were supposed to communicate with me through Eddie Guerrero, Clint," Elizabeth said. "I thought we made it clear there was to be no contact."

"That was before I knew you'd be in town, Elizabeth," he said.

"How did you know that?" she asked. "And how did you find me?"

"It's very hard for a woman who looks like you to stay hidden, don't you think?" he asked. "And as far as finding you, I just followed Eddie."

She looked at him, frowning and biting her lip. She folded her arms beneath her breasts and studied him. It was almost a posture of superiority, like the one she'd adopted with Eddie.

"Why are you here?" she asked him.

"I think the question that is more to the point, Elizabeth," he said, "is why are you here?"

"We were . . . concerned."

"It's only been a couple of days."

"We expected you to move faster."

"I never move without getting the lay of the land first," he explained. "But in fact, I ended up moving more quickly than I'd intended because of circumstances."

"The shooting, you mean?"

"What shooting would that be?"

"Someone took a shot—" she said, then bit her lip to stop herself from going any further.

"How'd you know someone took a shot at me?" he asked.

She bit her lip harder. A better liar would have gotten away with her next statement.

"I heard it . . . from Eddie."

"Elizabeth," he said, "you took a shot at me, didn't you? In fact, you took two."

She looked around the room as she tried to think of a good lie.

"Come on," Clint said. "A lie is not going to do either of us any good."

She stopped casting her eye around the room and looked directly at him.

"I wanted you to move faster," she said. "I wanted you to get the answers."

"And I did."

"You got the answer?"

"I moved faster," he said. "I rode out to the ranch to talk with . . . with the old man."

"Is it him?" she asked, anxiously. "Is he William Travis?"

"Elizabeth," he said, "I don't know."

"But you said you spoke with him."

"I did."

"What did he say?" she demanded. "When you asked him? Did he say he was or he wasn't William Travis of the Alamo?"

Clint hesitated. The old man had spoken to him willingly, had acted very much the gentleman. What would happen if he told Elizabeth what the old man had told him about not really remembering?

"Clint?"

"He didn't say," he answered.

"What?"

"He didn't say whether he was or wasn't Travis," Clint said. "As a matter of fact, before I could really get him talking I was looking at a dozen or so guns."

He told her what had happened, first with the ranch hands, and then when Cal Davis arrived.

"So . . . you still don't know?"

"That's right," Clint said. "I don't."

"So . . . what are you going to do?"

"I'm going to keep asking questions," he said.

"Well . . . I'll help."

"You can help by staying out of sight," he told her, "and by not taking any more shots at me."

She smiled and said, "I missed, didn't I?"

"Not by much."

"I'm very good with a gun," she said. "If I'd wanted to hurt you, I would have."

"Does your father know you're here?"

"He . . . he doesn't, no."

"Where does he think your are?"

"Gonzales."

"Then why are you here, Elizabeth?"

"I told you," she said. "I wanted you to move a little faster. I wanted you to find out—"

"Can I ask you a question, Elizabeth?"

"Go ahead."

"Do you believe him?"

"Who?" she asked. "My father, or Travis?"

"Either one," he said. "Do you believe that the old man is the real William Travis?"

She hesitated a moment, then said, "What I think doesn't matter. The only thing that matters is what my father thinks, and what you can find out."

Now it was Clint's turn to hesitate, before saying, "All right, then, Elizabeth, leave me alone and let me find out."

She walked up to him and stood just inches away; he could feel her heat.

"I can stay out of your way," she said, in a low, sexy voice, "without actually . . . leaving you alone."

THIRTY-SEVEN

Being in bed with Carmen and Rosa had been fun, but being in bed with Elizabeth Vargas was an experience. She was all wild hair and heaving, heavy breasts in his face as she sat astride him in her rooming house bed. Clint wondered if the other boarders could hear them, because neither of them was being quiet about what they were doing.

As her breasts swayed in front of him, he sought out her nipples with his mouth. His hands were on her hips as she bounced up and down on him, gasping and crying out each time she came down. She rode his rigid cock with abandon, eyes closed, had thrown back, sweat making her body gleam. Her nails dug into his chest, but he barely felt the pain. There was just too much pleasure going on at the same time. Finally, when her time came, she caught her breath, opened her eyes, stared down at him and then muffled her own screams of delight by smashing her mouth up against his and thrusting her tongue inside. In the midst of it, he upended her, put her on her back and rode her until he exploded inside her, bringing another group of moans and screams from her. After that, he collapsed on her and she—

apparently enjoying the weight of him on top of her—wrapped him in her arms and cooed to him in Spanish . . .

"The other boarders . . . ," he said later, breathlessly.

"There are no other boarders," she said, "and Mrs. Lopez, who runs this place, is almost totally deaf." She snuggled up against him and kissed his chest. "So there's no need to worry about bothering anyone else."

"Well," he said, "that's good to know, but it's time for me to go."

He slid his arm from beneath her head and sat up, swinging his feet to the floor.

"No, stay—" she started.

"Elizabeth," he said, cutting her off and reaching for his pants, "you're the one who said you wanted me to get your answers for you . . . for your father. As much as I like being in bed with you, I'm not going to find any answers here . . ." He turned and looked at her. "Or am I?"

"No," she said, "of course not."

"Then I have to go."

He stood up and dressed quickly while she watched, holding the sheet up to hide her nudity, which he found odd. During sex she had no shame, but after she seemed to get shy.

"What are you going to do?" she asked.

"I'm not sure." He strapped on his gun. "Somebody killed one of Cal Davis's men. Maybe I'll try to find out who that was."

"But why?" she asked. "What does that have to do with what we are trying to find out?"

"I don't know," he said. "Maybe the killer knows something that will help us."

·　·　·

Before Clint had gone to see Elizabeth Vargas at the rooming house where Eddie had led him, he'd asked Eddie if he'd found out anything about the murder.

"That I do not have any answers about, yet," Eddie admitted. "But I am still keeping my ears open."

"All right," Clint had said. "I might as well keep mine open, too."

"But since Señorita Vargas is in town," Eddie added, "maybe she had something to do with it?"

Clint had stared at the man and asked, "You think Elizabeth Vargas killed him?"

"I was joking, señor," Eddie said, hastily, "just joking."

Now, as Clint walked away from the rooming house, he wondered how much of a joke it might really have been. Elizabeth was proficient with guns. Maybe clubbing a man to death with one was something she was capable of, but the question would then be, why? But the fact that the man was employed by the man who might be William Travis was a little too much of a coincidence for him. Everything that was happening had to be tied in to whether or not the old man was actually Travis of the Alamo.

The answer to that question might supply the answers to all others.

THIRTY-EIGHT

Cal knew he had two choices. He could ask the old man what he had told Clint Adams, or ask Adams himself. The old man's mind went in and out, but Cal decided to see if he could pry some lucid information from him. Usually, the best way to do that was to scare him. It seemed to make his mind sharper.

Davis entered the office, and the old man looked up at him as he closed the door behind him.

"What can I do for you, Cal?"

"I'll tell you what, you old fool," Davis said. "Tell me what you talked to Clint Adams about yesterday."

"Adams," the older man repeated. "Did I meet a man by that name yester—"

Davis didn't let him finish. He came around the desk and grabbed the man by the front of his shirt.

"Listen to me!" he snapped. "You better start answering my questions or you're gonna find yourself back where you were when I found you."

The man known as William Travis frowned and asked, "B-back in the street?"

"That's right."

"I don't want to go back in the street, Cal."

"Then tell me what you and Adams talked about."

Abruptly, the man's expression changed from one of fear to indignation. He grabbed Cal's wrist and said, "There's no need to get physical Cal. I'll tell you."

Davis could see by the look in the man's eyes that he was suddenly all there. He released his shirt.

"All right, then," he said. "I'm listening . . ."

"You goin' into town alone?" Bob Gregg asked.

"No." Cal Davis pulled the cinch tight on his saddle and ducked away when the horse bucked once. "Get the men ready. You're all comin' in with me."

"All the hands?"

"Not the cowpunchers," Cal said. "Just the gunhands."

"What are we goin' in for?"

"I'm gonna talk to Clint Adams," Davis said. "I want to see if his story matches the ol—Mr. Travis's story."

"What happens if he throws down on you?"

"That would be interestin'," Davis said, "but I don't think it's gonna happen." Finished with the saddle, he turned to face the other man. "But if it does, you boys will be backin' me up."

"You decided yet who's gonna replace Jackson?"

"No," Davis said, mounting up, "I'm still thinkin' about it. Why, Bob, you want the job?"

"I'll take it."

"We'll see," Davis said. "Maybe when we get back . . . but get the men ready to move now."

Clint walked over to the sheriff's office and entered. Sheriff Strode was seated behind his desk. Neither of his deputies was around.

"Good morning, Sheriff."

"Adams," Strode said. "What can I do for you?"

"I was just wondering if you had made any progress on the murder," Clint asked.

"No," Strode said, with a scowl, "I don't know any more today than I knew yesterday. What about you?"

"What about me?"

"You had a talk with Travis yesterday," the lawman said. "What did you find out?"

"Not much."

"Talk about the Alamo at all?"

"The Alamo?" Clint asked. "Why would I talk to him about the Alamo?"

"You know they call him the Ghost of Goliad, don't you?" Strode asked. "He claims he's the same Travis who was at the Alamo."

"You ever hear him claim that?" Clint asked.

"Never heard him say it himself," Strode admitted, "but plenty of others have."

"Like who?"

"Cal Davis, for one."

"Davis works for Travis," Clint said. "Maybe it's in his best interest to make people think what he wants them to think."

"You sayin' it's all a lie?"

"Could be, couldn't it?"

"I suppose," Strode said, rubbing his jaw. "You think that has somethin' to do with Jackson being killed?"

"I don't know anything about anything, Sheriff," Clint said. "I was just making an inquiry."

"Just curious?"

"That's right."

"So you don't care if the man is really Travis or not," Strode said.

"It's no skin off my nose who he is, Sheriff," Clint said, "but it sure does seem a hot topic in town. Seems Goliad's kind of split on the subject. What do you think?"

"I ain't paid to think," Strode said, "leastways not about that."

THIRTY-NINE

Cal Davis rode into Goliad with five of his gunnies while Clint was still in the sheriff's office.

"Let me get this straight, Cal," Bob Gregg said, as they dismounted at the livery. "We're here to kill The Gunsmith . . . today?"

"That's right."

"Any particular reason?"

"I have a reason," Davis said. "You and the boys are involved because you'll be gettin' paid. You think that's reason enough for you and them?"

"Depends on how much we're getting' paid, I guess."

"Well, let me put it to you this way, Bob," Davis said. "The less you get them to take, the more you'll get."

"And Lex's job?"

"Sure," Davis said, "why not? You'll be top hand."

"That wasn't exactly Lex's job, Cal," Gregg said.

"Don't worry, Bob," Davis said. "I'll let you know exactly what Lex's job was, when this is all over."

"Okay," Gregg said. "I'll talk to the boys. They'll want to know if Mr. Travis is all for this."

"This is exactly what Mr. Travis wants," Davis said. "You can tell them that. When they're all ready, meet me at Anderson's."

"We'll be there."

In point of fact, Lex Jackson's actual job was as Cal Davis's confidante. Jackson had been the only man working for Davis who knew where Cal had picked up the old man. What Davis had to decide was whether or not he needed another confidante. Did he really need for someone else to know what he knew?

What he didn't need was for Clint Adams to be asking any more questions about "William Travis."

Steve Collins was heading to the sheriff's office when he spotted the men from the Travis ranch walking across the street. These were boys who would not be in town without Cal Davis.

As Collins approached the sheriff's office, the door opened and Clint Adams stepped out. Both men stopped when they saw each other.

"I think we got trouble brewin' in town," Collins warned him. "I saw some of Cal Davis's boys."

"So?"

"They're the boys he uses when he's lookin' for trouble," the deputy said. "And they were all friends of Lex Jackson's."

"That's got nothing to do with me," Clint said. "I wasn't involved in the man's death."

"I don't think they'll care," Collins said. "If Davis sends them after you, that's all they'll need to know."

"Why are you telling me all this?"

"Because you talked to Travis yesterday," Collins said. "If he told you something you shouldn't know, Cal Davis ain't gonna like it."

"You mean like if he told me he wasn't really William Travis of the Alamo?"

"Did he tell you that?"

"Not exactly." Clint decided to confide in Collins. "Let's get off the street."

"Where to?"

"Anderson's?"

"I think those boys were headed there," Collins said.

"The cantina, then," Clint said. "Come on. I'll buy you a beer."

"Buy me a cup of coffee instead," Collins said. "It's a little early for beer."

"Not for me," Clint said. After spending the night with Rosa and Carmen, and then the morning in bed with Elizabeth Vargas, he was in need of something stronger than coffee.

As it turned out, Clint had coffee *and* beer while Steve Collins just had coffee.

They entered the cantina and found only the barman and one other customer. Neither Rosa nor Carmen was in sight. Clint liked to think that both of them were catching up on some sleep.

"Okay," Collins said, when they were seated at a table with a pot of coffee, two cups, and a beer for Clint.

"He doesn't know."

"What?"

"The old man," Clint said. "He doesn't know if he's Travis or not."

"How could he not know?"

Clint shrugged.

"He's old," he said. "His memory is not what it used to be. Maybe he is Travis, or maybe Cal Davis has just told him that he is."

"Why would Davis do that?"

"To make money," Clint said. "Somehow, he's got to be making money out of this."

"It's the old man who owns the ranch," Collins said. "And some businesses in town."

"Maybe it is, and maybe it isn't," Clint said. "What if Davis is just using the old man as a front? Setting him up as this legend from the Alamo?"

"Then he's not gonna like it that the old man told you he can't remember."

"No, he's not."

"Maybe that's why he's here with his men," Collins said. "Maybe the old man told him."

"If he did, and Davis and his men are looking for me, you better stay out of the way,"

"I'm the law."

"You think the sheriff, or Deputy Madison, would stand with me against them?"

"Not a chance."

"Then why would you?"

"Because I'm not them," Collins said. "Because I ain't gonna stand around while they gun you, one to six. That's got nothin' to do with me wearin' this badge—but it just so happens that I am wearin' it."

"You think that's going to matter to them?"

"No," Collins said, "but it's gonna matter to me, Clint."

"Two to six?" Clint asked. "You like those odds better?"

"When you're one of the two?" Collins asked. "I like them odds a lot better."

FORTY

When Cal Davis entered the sheriff's office, Strode was no gladder to see him than he had been to see Clint Adams.

"What do you want, Cal?"

"Just a friendly warnin', Sheriff," Davis said. "Stay off the street today."

Strode glared at Davis. "You got your boys with you today?"

"I do."

"So you're lookin' for trouble."

"Actually," Davis said, "I'm lookin' to avoid trouble."

"And for that I have to stay off the street?"

"Like I said," Davis replied, "I just wanted to give you a friendly warnin'."

"Say," Strode said, "this wouldn't have anythin' to do with Jackson's death, would it? Did you find out who did it?"

"I don't have a clue who did it," Davis said, "and this ain't got nothin' to do with Jackson."

Strode hesitated, then asked, "So it's Adams, isn't it? You and your boys, you're goin' after The Gunsmith."

"Just stay off the street, Sheriff," Davis said. "It's for your own good."

As Davis headed for the door, Strode stood up quickly.

"Cal," he said, "I can't just let you gun a man down in the street. It's my job to see that kind of thing never happens."

Davis turned and faced the sheriff.

"You wouldn't have this job if it wasn't for . . . Mr. Travis, you know?" he said. "He pays you."

"I work for the town."

"Mr. Travis *is* the town, Andy," Davis said. "You haven't forgotten that, have you?"

"Cal—"

"Just stay off the street, Andy," Davis said. "Don't take a hand in this."

This time Davis made it out the door without Strode stopping him, but the lawman walked to the window to look outside. Davis stepped off the boardwalk and headed in the direction of Anderson's saloon. Strode imagined that his men might be waiting for him there.

He left the window and went behind his desk to collect his gunbelt and hat. He had no idea where Clint Adams might have gotten to, but the man at least deserved a warning.

Clint and Steve Collins were coming out of the cantina when the sheriff saw them. He crossed the street and called out Clint's name, but directed his first comment to his deputy when he reached them.

"What are you doin', Steve?"

"I saw some of Davis's boys in town," Collins said. "I thought I should let Cl—Adams know."

Strode looked at Clint and said, "Actually that's why I was lookin' for you, too. I just talked with Cal Davis at my office. He and his men are lookin' for you."

"What for?"

Strode had to word this carefully. He couldn't afford to let it seem that he was condoning gunplay.

"It must have been somethin' you said yesterday," he commented. "Did you get on Cal's wrong side?"

"Sheriff," Clint said, "I don't think Cal Davis has a right side. You're trying to say they're looking for me to kill me."

"Well . . . they're not just gonna shoot you down in the street," Strode said.

"Why? Because you'd stop them?"

"Look, Adams—"

"So they're going to goad me so it looks like a fair fight? Six against one?"

"Two," Collins said, "six against two."

Strode looked at his deputy. "What?"

"I'm standin' with Clint against Davis and his men, Sheriff," Collins said. "I can't just watch . . . and neither can you."

Strode squared off with his deputy. "Are you tryin' to tell me how to do my job?"

"Somebody should," Collins said. "You're the sheriff for the town, Andy, not William Travis and Cal Davis."

Strode glared at Collins this time, his face growing more red by the minute.

Finally he said, "Steve, if you're gonna take part in a street fight, you can do it without that badge."

"You're right," Collins said. "I can."

He took off the badge and held it out to Strode, fighting the urge to drop it in the street. Strode took the badge and closed his hand into a fist around it.

"You boys kill anybody in this town and I'll lock you up."

Collins smiled, reached into his pocket, took out a federal marshal's badge and pinned it on.

"What the hell—" Strode said.

"Sheriff," Clint said, "meet Marshal William J. Mac-Donald."

Strode stared first at Clint, and then at Marshal Mac-Donald.

"I don't understand."

"It's simple," MacDonald said. "I was sent in here to investigate you."

"Me? For what?"

"You'll find out after I send in my report," MacDonald said. "For now, I'd advise you to enjoy wearin' that badge. You might not be wearin' it much longer."

Strode glared at MacDonald, tightened his hand around the deputy's badge he was holding, then turned and stalked away.

"I was wondering when you were going to come out from undercover," Clint said.

"I want to thank you for goin' along, Clint," MacDonald said. "I was worried you might blow my cover when you first walked in."

"So what's next, Marshal?"

"My job is about over, I think," MacDonald said. "Sheriff Strode is obviously in the pocket of either Cal Davis or the man he works for, who may or may not be William Travis of the Alamo."

"Is that why you were here?" Clint asked. "Because of Strode working for Travis?"

"Is Travis why you are here?"

Clint decided that if Marshal MacDonald was going to stand with him against Cal Davis and five men he might as well know the truth.

"I was asked to come and find out if Travis was the real deal," Clint said. "Travis of the Alamo."

"I was sent in for a couple of reasons," MacDonald said. "I was supposed to check on Strode, and on Cal Davis and his employer. The whole 'Ghost of Goliad' business is of federal interest."

"So our jobs have crossed," Clint said, "but are we at cross-purposes?"

"I don't think so," MacDonald said. "I think we should find Davis and his men and see how far they want to take this. After that, I'm gonna have Strode removed as sheriff, and we'll take a real close look at Travis's business practices."

"Does it mater if he's *the* William Travis?"

"A lot of people in government feel that the memory of the Alamo is sacred," MacDonald said. "Whether he's the real one or not, he's tradin' on that. It's got to stop, one way or another."

"Have you talked to Travis yourself?"

"No," MacDonald said, "but now that I'm wearin' my real badge, it might be about time."

"We're probably going to have to go through Cal Davis and his guns for that to happen."

"Well," MacDonald said, "up to now I hadn't had anyone who could back me in that kind of play."

"Then if we're going to do it," Clint said, "we might as well do it."

FORTY-ONE

Cal Davis met with his men at Anderson's saloon.

"Everybody have a drink," he told them. "We're goin' after The Gunsmith."

One of the men cleared his throat and asked, "Are we gettin' paid extra for facin' him?"

"Paid extra?" Davis asked. "What about the reputation you'll have as one of the men who killed him?"

"Six against one?" another man asked. "Not much of a rep there. Me, I'll take cash money."

"I think they're right, Cal," Gregg said. "You want us to back you against Adams, you'll have to come up with some money."

Davis poured himself a glass of whiskey, downed it and glared at his men. There were no other patrons in the place, as they had all fled when Gregg and the four other men entered. Only Anderson remained at his station behind the bar.

"Is this what you all say?" Davis asked.

The men nodded and Gregg said, "I'm afraid so."

"Then the rep for killin' The Gunsmith will be mine," Davis said, "and only mine."

"That's fine," Gregg said.

"Then it's agreed," Davis said. "You'll all be paid extra for killin' The Gunsmith."

"He's got to be dead for us to collect?" Gregg asked.

"He's got to be dead."

Gregg looked at the other men, who all nodded.

"Then let's drink on it," he said, and they all bellied up to the bar.

Clint and Marshal MacDonald came walking down the center of Main Street as Cal Davis and his men came out of Anderson's.

"Well, well . . . ," Clint said. "We won't have to go looking for them, after all."

"Fate," MacDonald said.

"I like that a hell of a lot better than coincidence," Clint said.

"Wait," Cal Davis said, when he spotted Clint and Mac-Donald.

"Who's that?" Gregg asked.

"The deputy," Davis said. "Collins."

"That's no deputy's badge on his chest," Gregg said.

"No, it ain't," Davis said. "You wait here with the men."

Davis stepped down into the street and approached Clint and MacDonald.

"Cal," MacDonald said.

"What's goin' on, Steve?" Davis asked. "What's that badge doin' on your chest?"

"This is the one I'm supposed to be wearin'," Mac-Donald said. "The name's William MacDonald, federal marshal."

"What was the idea of goin' by Steve Collins?"

"Just doin' my job, Cal," the marshal said.

"Why are you standin' with Adams?"

"Also doin' my job," MacDonald said. "I've got to ride out and have a talk with your boss."

"I can't let you do that."

"And I guess that's why I'm standin' with Adams," MacDonald said. "I've to go through you to get to Travis, right?"

"Right."

"Then let's do it," MacDonald said. "Two against six probably doesn't faze you any more than one against six did."

"One, two," Davis said. "It don't much matter to me."

"That's pretty much what I said," MacDonald replied.

"So we do it right out here in the street?"

"Where else?" MacDonald asked.

"I've got to go back to my men."

"We're not going to shoot you in the back, Davis," Clint said. "You go back and tell them they have to face two of us, now."

Davis eyed both of them for a moment, then started backing away. Eventually, he turned and walked to his men.

"Shoulda shot him in the back," MacDonald said.

"Naw," Clint said. "It's better this way."

"Yeah," MacDonald said, "I guess."

"Any idea how good Davis is?" Clint asked. "Or any of his men?"

"He's supposed to be pretty good," MacDonald said. "The rest are just hired guns."

"Okay," Clint said, "then I'll take Davis."

"And I get the other five?" MacDonald asked.

"Let's see how they line up," Clint said, "before we decide that."

• • •

"We takin' the two of 'em?" Gregg asked. "Even the deputy?"

"He's not a deputy, he's a marshal," Davis said, "and yeah, both of them."

"A marshal?" Gregg asked. "For real?"

"Yeah, for real."

Gregg thought a moment, then asked, "We get extra for the marshal, right?"

FORTY-TWO

When they stepped off the boardwalk and into the street, Cal Davis was standing with three men on his left and two to his right.

"I'll take Cal and the two to his left," Clint said. "You take the two on your right."

"His left? My right?" MacDonald asked. "That leaves one man, don't it? The one on his far left?"

"He's up for grabs," Clint said.

"What?"

Clint had heard the term once before—in San Francisco, maybe.

"Whoever finishes first gets him."

"Listen," MacDonald said, "I'm gonna shoot and move."

"What?"

"After my first shot," MacDonald said, "I'm gonna move."

"Won't that throw off your second shot?"

"Maybe," the marshal said, "but it'll throw theirs off, too."

"Well," Clint said, "you do what you've got to do to survive."

"That was my thought, exactly."

As the six men approached them, Clint and the marshal stopped talking and moved to put a little more space between them and the oncoming gang.

In the sheriff's office, both Strode and Deputy Madison were watching from the window.

"Ain't we gonna do nothin', Sheriff?" Madison asked.

"No."

"But there's only two of them."

"One of them is the Gunsmith, boy," Strode said. "They'll do okay."

"I gotta go out—" Madison said, starting to move toward the door, but the older man stopped him by grabbing his arm.

"You go out there you'll get killed," he said. "Just stay where you are, damn it!"

"Well . . . are we at least gonna arrest the last one's standin'?"

"Kid," Strode said, "with any luck they'll just all kill each other."

The talking was over.

The first man to move was Davis. He went for his gun with every intention of killing Clint Adams. Before he could clear leather, though, he saw a puff of smoke from Clint's gun and felt the impact of the bullet in his chest. He didn't feel much after that—at least, nothing after he said, "Oh shit," and hit the ground.

Clint moved his guns then and fired two more times. The two men on Davis's left went down like tin can targets on a fence—*boom*, *boom*, onto their backs, one gun in the dirt and the other still in its holster.

Clint turned his attention to the others. Apparently, moving after the first shot had helped MacDonald. He was lying on his belly in the street, very much alive, while two men were laying in the street, their guns in the dirt next to them.

That left the sixth man, Bob Gregg, standing alone. Neither Clint nor MacDonald fired at him, each waiting for the other one to do it.

"Wait! Wait!" Gregg shouted, throwing his hands in the air.

MacDonald got to his feet and looked at Clint.

"You finished first," he said. "He was yours."

"I thought I'd leave him to you," Clint said, "even things out."

"I'm not that competitive," MacDonald said. "I wouldn't have minded if you got four to my two."

Clint shrugged and said, "Should have told me that when we started."

MacDonald shook his head and approached the man who was holding his hands in the air.

After leaving Bob Gregg with Sheriff Strode to put in his jail—"And he better still be here when I get back," Mac-Donald had warned—Clint and the marshal rode out to the Travis ranch. Since Davis had taken all his gunmen with him, there was no one to stop them from entering the house.

"This way," Clint said, leading MacDonald down a hall. "Let's try his study."

They found the old man there, seated behind his desk with his chin on his chest.

"Dead?" MacDonald asked.

"Asleep, I think," Clint said.

He approached the man, not wanting to startle him awake, but he needn't have bothered. When he touched him, the man didn't move, at all.

"You were right," Clint said. "He's dead."

He went back to stand next to MacDonald, and they both stared at the dead man behind the desk.

"So . . . was he Travis of the Alamo?"

"He didn't know," Clint said. "If he was, he'd forgotten it a long time ago."

"So there's no proof either way?"

"Scar over his eye," Clint said, "but that could be from anything."

"So what do we do now?"

"Send for the doctor," Clint said, "and the undertaker."

"What about your job?" MacDonald asked. "Proving who he was?"

"Guess that's not going to get done," Clint said. "Don Carlos Vargas will have to live out the rest of his days not knowing."

"Don Carlos, huh?" MacDonald said. "Heard his daughter's real pretty."

"Gorgeous."

They stood there silently for a few moments, then Clint asked, "What about Lex Jackson?"

"What about him?"

"Who killed him?"

"Damned if I know," MacDonald said. "Ain't my job to find out. Let Strode do it. Maybe it's the last thing he'll do before I have him removed from office."

Clint shook his head. "This isn't a very satisfying end to all this."

"Speak for yourself," MacDonald said. "I've been wantin' this job to end for weeks."

"Where do you go from here?"

"Away," MacDonald said, "just away. What about you?"

"Well," Clint said, "I guess that doesn't sound so bad. I'll pass the word to Don Carlos and be on my way, too."

"Poor old guy," Clint Adams said. "Must be hell dyin' and not knowin' who you are."

He'd always thought being shot in the back was the worst way to die, but maybe this was worse.

AUTHOR'S NOTE

In 1891 William J. MacDonald was commissioned as a captain in the Texas Rangers and went on to become one of the most famous of the Rangers. His motto was: "No man in the wrong can stand up against a fellow that's in the right and keeps on acomin'." He's also believed to be the inspiration behind the "One man, one riot," legend. A Ranger arrives in a town to put down a riot and, when asked where the others are, replies, "There's only one riot."

Watch for

THE REAPERS

287th novel in the exciting GUNSMITH series

from Jove

Coming in November!

REMEMBER THE ALAMO?

Beautiful Elizabeth Vargas may dress like a man, but to Clint Adams she's all woman. Her charms aren't the only reason he agrees to meet her father, Don Carlos, though. How can he pass up an opportunity to speak to a man who might just be the last survivor of the Battle of the Alamo?

Don Carlos wants Clint to suss out a man in nearby Goliad who claims to be Captain William Travis. And he's not just living in the town—he's running it, or at least his foreman is. But Travis took a bullet to the forehead at the Alamo, and Santa Anna himself identified the body. Are the good folks of Goliad seeing ghosts?

OVER FIVE MILLION GUNSMITH BOOKS IN PRINT!

www.penguin.com

ISBN 0-515-14020-1

$5.50 U.S.
$8.50 CAN